Haunts

A Novel
George Jansen

Published by

Fool Church Media

Eugene, Oregon

Haunts
Copyright © 2018 George Jansen

First Edition 2018, Fool Church Media

Paperback ISBN: 978-1-945232-32-9
Epub ISBN: 978-1-945232-33-6
Kindle ISBN: 978-1-945232-34-3
Audio Book ISBN: 978-1-945232-35-0
Google Book ISBN: 978-1-945232-36-7
Hardback ISBN: 978-1-945232-37-4

Manufactured/Printed in the United States of America
Printed 2018, Fool Church Media
Shelve under:
     Literary Fiction
     Literary Romance Fiction

Reviews

"Haunts takes you on an unforgettable journey into the seedy underbelly of San Francisco, a world populated by winos, drug addicts, and prophetic ghosts that pop up with the regularity of the morning mail. As compelling as it is stark, as absorbing as it is repellent, it is one of those rare books that forfeits the safety of convention to tell its story in blood. In places, it reminds me of Hemingway's The Sun Also Rises; in other places it is reminiscent of Fellini's Satyricon."

James Hanna, author of *Call Me Pomeroy, The Siege, A Second Less Capable Head*

"Down-and-out street person George Zumpo personifies San Francisco's Tenderloin district, a neighborhood most natives and tourists do their best to avoid. With deep compassion for his unforgettable characters, George Jansen breathes life into Zumpo and an offbeat cast each of whom carries a personal load of faded ambitions and diminishing hope. In Haunts, readers are treated to a captivating story in which they will discover a common humanity with Zumpo and his ongoing struggle to make sense of his life."

Alfred J. Garrotto, author of *There's More: A Novella of Life and Afterlife*

"Jansen pulls you into the lives of his on-the-edge-of-sanity characters who populate 1970s San Francisco's SOMA—South of Market. The City was filled with people compelled to leave their origins in search of something different—but what? Find out when Haunts spins everyone on the wheel of Fortune."

Elana O'Loskey, *Staff Writer/Columnist, The Orinda News*

Cover Art

The cover image was taken by photographer Bryan Costales, inside *The Warehouse Cafe* in Port Costa, California back in 2008. Granted, this is long after 1976, but the author felt this image reminded him of the flavor of the old building on Natoma Street in San Francisco.

For Laura

one

In December of the year 1975 a half-breed, in the parlance of the day, marched into the City by the Golden Gate. His name was George Zumpo, and he wore the navy blue greatcoat he'd gotten when he was a recruit in the Salvation Army. A pack was strapped to his back. A greasy orange sleeping bag was tied above that. On his head was a black Stetson cowboy hat. An eagle feather he'd gotten at a pawnshop in Reno, "The Biggest Little City in World" was stuck in the headband. He wore steel-toed boots that were snug and good, but he'd walked so far his feet were killing him.

To Zumpo, it was not Christmas but the time of the Winter Solstice, and he'd been on the road for days. He'd hitched, walked and frozen all the way across the bitter Sierra: Dresslerville, Gardnerville, Mottsville, Woodfords. He'd visited cousins in Markleeville and learned that his wife, Leela, was somewhere in this big, concrete city. She'd run off with a rat named Charlie Weasel when Zumpo was ensconced in the Douglas County Jail. Charlie had also stolen his pure white German Shepherd named White Dog and his 1965 Volkswagen Westfalia camper that had curtains in the windows.

There were white people all around him and so many buildings that his vision was blocked no matter which way he looked. Cars and buses idled in the street. He saw an orderly line of orderly white people at a bus stop. The women all wore plastic rain boots and clear, plastic raincoats. A trolley bus opened its doors and swallowed some up. There was one woman with cat eyes who gave him a nervous glance then turned away. Zumpo didn't want to frighten any women, so he tapped the shoulder of a man in a thin raincoat that wouldn't have been much use on a winter's night on the eastern slope.

"Excuse me, sir," Zumpo said in his least threatening tone. "Do you know where there's a mission around here?"

The man had a beard trimmed so perfectly it reminded Zumpo of a rich man's lawn. "A mission? Like Mission Dolores?" the man said. He had a faggy voice.

Zumpo shook his head. "No, I don't think so." And got away from him as quick as he could.

Near the front of the line was a young man who wore a quilted, down jacket, and Zumpo figured he might at least have some common sense.

Zumpo said, "Is there a mission around here, my friend?"

"A rescue mission, you mean?" The young man had golden hair that went down the nape of his neck and curled over the collar of his jacket. He reminded Zumpo of George Custer, the egomaniac who got his balls cut off by Zumpo's cousins, the Lakota, at the Battle of the Greasy Grass.

"Yes. A rescue mission," Zumpo said. "Jesus Saves and so on and so forth, Amen."

Yellowhair gave his head a nod then pointed out the path. "Go straight up Market to Sixth. Turn left and go a few more blocks. There are some, but it's a bit of a walk."

"I like walking," Zumpo told him.

"Not me," Yellowhair said. He took a step towards Zumpo, and Zumpo saw that he was lame.

"I have walked all the way here from Dresslerville in Nevada," Zumpo said, "to rescue my wife from a Weasel."

"Is that so," Yellowhair said. "There's snow up there, you know."

"Not so deep," Zumpo said.

In the days before the whites came, Zumpo's people spent their whole lives walking: to the lake and the fish runs when the snows melted, to the rabbit hunt in the spring, across the valley floor in summer, to the pine nut harvest in the fall.

Zumpo was a forager too. "Could you spare some change?"

Yellowhair reached right down into the pocket of his pants like there was nothing to it and pulled out a quarter, three dimes, a nickel, and two pennies. He gave them all to Zumpo, sixty-two cents. He pointed a finger at a little bottle of pear wine that was poorly concealed in the pocket of Zumpo's Salvation Army greatcoat.

"Don't spend it all on Ripple," he said.

Zumpo's first impulse was to tell him he'd spend it on whatever the fuck he wanted. But he was through with saying things like that; he was the new Zumpo. He pulled the bottle out of his pocket.

"Wine is part of my heritage." Zumpo was one-half *Wa-she-shu*, three-eighths *Siciliano*, and one-eighth *Numu*. "Want a shot?"

Yellowhair thought for a moment, took the bottle, wiped the spout with the palm of his hand and drank. At least he was not afraid of redskin cooties.

Zumpo had wandered to many places with his pack on his back and his boots on his feet and White Dog trotting along before him: the Sangre de Cristo, the Mountains of the Moon, the Crow Agency. In Death Valley Jesus had spoken to him, and the sun had turned his

3

brain to snakes, but he had never seen a more desolate place than this city. All along his line of march the tall buildings, the buses, taxis, and streetcars hemmed him in. Countless vans and countless trucks loaded and unloaded bottles of water, cartons of Doritos, boxes of paper, and every which way he turned more and more and more people hemmed him in. He held his breath against the claustrophobic air, found a place inside the angle where two big buildings joined and took the bottle of Ripple out of his pocket.

The white man's god of Christmas stood a few feet away, dressed in his red suit and false beard, ringing his brass bell.

"Merry Christmas. Merry Christmas."

"Merry Chris-my-ass," Zumpo called, but Santa was too stupid to get the joke.

There were "Walk/Don't Walk" signals on every corner and signs of every description: "No Left Turn," "No Right Turn," "No U Turn." There were pretty women too, but when it began to drizzle they all sprouted colored umbrellas and hid their heads inside.

At Sixth Street he turned left, as Yellowhair had advised, and all at once the territory grew kinder. No more stainless steel. No more fake brick sidewalks, just rain and beggars and police cars. There were old hotels that advertised weekly rates, dark bars that smelled of alcohol and loud talk, liquor stores, pawnshops, laundromats.

Just before a little alley, he saw a sign overhanging the sidewalk. It had a blue cross in its center. The word "SOMA" was spelled out in big letters and below the cross itself were the words "South of Market Mission." Half a dozen men stood in front of its closed doors, lined up along its painted-out, storefront window. Zumpo took a place at the end of the line and asked the white man in front of him what was on the menu tonight.

"Sermons and spaghetti," the white man told him. "Got an extra smoke?"

Zumpo gave him one. The white man thanked him and began to laugh. Zumpo didn't know why, but still, he laughed along with him.

Straight across Sixth Street there was a little park with asphalt paths through the dirt where big concrete conduits painted in pastels were set up on stocky concrete legs. When the doors of the mission finally opened men crawled out of the conduits like pocket gophers climbing out of their holes in the ground. Some wore heavy coats, some green army fatigue jackets, and others just cotton jackets and baseball caps. They crossed Sixth Street wherever they pleased, disdainful of the law, jaywalking but struggling like cripples or old men.

"Welcome. Welcome to SOMA Mission." A Chinese-American man stood at the open door as Zumpo trooped in with all the rest. The Chinese man was dressed in a black shirt with a clerical collar like a priest but he was young, good-looking and still slender.

He smiled. "Welcome to SOMA Mission."

Zumpo said, "Father forgive me for I have not sinned."

The Chinese priest laughed. "I'm not a Catholic. I'm Pastor Jimmy Huang." He put out his hand to shake and Zumpo took it. He asked Zumpo his name, and Zumpo told him.

Jimmy Huang laughed. "Zumpo? What kind of name is Zumpo? Did you escape from a circus?"

"You might say that."

Zumpo followed the shambling men into a room full of what looked like pews, but they were not sturdy, dark, oak pews like in a church. They were light, pinewood pews and only shellacked. Zumpo took a seat at the far end of one that was as near to the back of the room as he could get. He took the pack off his back and set it on the floor with his feet pressed up against it as proof against thieves. A man in a wheelchair was in the aisle beside him, and Zumpo asked him when they'd get the spaghetti. The man shushed Zumpo with a crooked finger at his lips then pointed it towards the front of the room where a Chinese woman, dressed just like Pastor Jimmy Huang, stood at a podium on a low riser.

"Good evening," she said. "I bring you a message of hope."

When the food finally came, it was on trays and they had to eat sitting in the plywood pews like savages rather than at proper tables. Still, it was fat and good: macaroni and cheese, garlic bread, and four hard boiled eggs—two white, two brown. When Zumpo was done eating he strapped on his pack again and went to the door. Pastor Jimmy shook his hand and told him that, regrettably, the men's dormitory was already full for the night.

"But we have a nice breakfast every morning. Come back if you wish."

Outside, the rain had begun again. Zumpo had camped out many times in worse places than a rainy city. Still, he went into a tiny grocery store on the corner of Sixth and Natoma and bought a bottle of Night Train fortified wine, partly for sustenance, partly because Yellowhair, a man who had given him sixty-two cents, had told him not to buy Ripple. When he stepped outside again he opened the wine and took a swig. Ripple was made from pears, that was sure, but a black man without any front teeth once told him that Night Train was made of Clorox and Kool-Aid.

"They wanna turn us white inside," the black man had said.

"We're already white inside," Zumpo told him.

When he took a second swig he thought he heard music. He listened again carefully and, when there were no cars roaring by, he could make out electric guitars and drums and a thumping bass echoing up a long, concrete canyon. Natoma was a one-way street but just one lane wide, and there were automobiles parked with their wheels up on the curbs making the sidewalks nearly impassable: an old Ford that had lost its grill, a Chevy Nova with flat feet, a round-eyed Volkswagen.

The music Zumpo heard was that of the great Howlin' Wolf's "Little Red Rooster." It seemed to be coming from somewhere down Natoma, but it wasn't Howlin' Wolf singing at all. Howlin' Wolf sounded like a Caterpillar tractor. This singer was more like a Toyota Corolla.

The rain came harder now, and the north winds blew. Zumpo found a wooden loading dock for light trucks that served a Goodwill store. It was only the height of a poker table like those at the Golden Horseshoe in Reno, but it was made of good wood and hollow underneath. Zumpo bent down. It was dark under the dock, but he could see wet trash, old newspapers, empty wine bottles, and food wrappers. He didn't smell rat, so he took off his big hat, slipped off his pack, and crawled under.

He didn't see the old man until the old man spoke.

"Hey! Get the fuck outta here. What the fuck. I hit that guy. You saw how I hit that guy. I can break your fuckin' jaw and don't think I won't. You get outta here."

The old man had a dirty gray beard and skinny fingers like twigs. He was wrapped around a bottle of Cisco Red, a wine that had a flavor like cough syrup, and a bouquet reminiscent of Trix cereal.

"Calm down brother," Zumpo said. "Listen to the music. Have a smoke."

He reached an open hand towards the old man, waited to make sure the old man wasn't afraid, then reached behind the old man's head and pulled a cigarette out of his ear. The old man took it and grinned like a Christmas baby.

"How the hell did you do that? How the hell?"

7

Zumpo and the old man smoked cigarettes, drank wine, listened to the blues of Howlin' Wolf and the rock of Bo Diddley, which roared down the alley. They chatted about the smog-drenched city of Los Angeles, where the old man had lived before his job and his unemployment ran out. They laughed about the concrete banks of the Los Angeles River where Zumpo had once made a dry camp. They talked of the DTs, compared hallucinations and found they had much in common.

Zumpo told the old man about Lake Tahoe, the rabbit hunt, and the Pine Nut Forest, which didn't exist anymore, cut down by the whites in the previous century. He told him about Charlie Weasel who had stolen his beautiful wife, and how he would find her and take her back home with him.

"Back to the reservation?" the old man said.

"No way," Zumpo said.

The old man passed out first, but Zumpo wasn't far behind. Just before he fell asleep in his orange sleeping bag, greasy as Greasy Grass, he thought of his wife and his dog and his Volkswagen Westfalia camper. As he drifted away he dreamed of them all driving back home and camping by the steaming hot springs of the Carson Valley.

two

In this same December of 1975 it just so happened that Christmas fell on a Thursday, and on Wednesday, in the financial district of the City, the Christmas parties started at noon—the bourgeoisie at Tadich Grill, the Ritz Poodle Dog, John's Steak House; the proletariat having to settle for the Royal Exchange, Schroeders, and Harrington's, where the party had already spilled out the doors and onto Front Street.

"They're not going to make you work on Friday are they?"

"God no. And even the people who have to work aren't actually going to *work*. Know what I mean?"

On the corner of California and Davis, warmed by a thin winter sun two young women in Mrs. Claus costumes—short red dresses with white trim, Santa style hats, and dark glasses—passed out sample packs of cigarettes. A brass quartet—trumpet, two French horns, and a trombone—pumped out Christmas carols while a cable car, decked out in Christmas green and red, rumbled up from the turntable at Market and Drumm clanging it's bell.

Hidden in the cold shadows of the loading dock behind the Consolidated Bank building, three dismounted bike messengers and a snowman with his head tucked underneath his arm, smoked pot and swigged Coca-Cola.

"Hey Frosty. Don't Bogart that joint, my friend ..."

High above on the twenty-eighth floor, clean, white light poured in through the glass walls of Consolidated's Word Processing Department. There, a young woman named Robin Jenks sat behind her IBM Mag Card Word Processor and waited. The corporate secretary had called down earlier and said that a letter to the regional presidents had to go out today and asked Robin's porky boss, Betty Schoenfield, if they had someone who could handle the job. Betty had volunteered Robin.

Forty-six minutes later, Robin's phone rang. She pushed a flashing button. "Word Processing," she said.

"Robin!" It was Sheila McCarthy, half drunk and sounding incredibly happy. "We're all down at Harrington's. The whole damn Programming Department. Most of Customer Service, too. Santa is passing out cigarettes. Free cigarettes! Can you believe it? Whole packs of them, and guys are buying me drinks! You got to get down here."

Robin said, "May I put you on hold for a moment?"

"Can't you talk?" Sheila said.

"Please hold," Robin told her. Fat Betty, wearing the green and red of the season, sat immobile in her glass cubicle watching over an empty department.

Robin stayed on her perch in Word Processing until almost three o'clock, when the corporate secretary called down again, said the letter wasn't going out after all, and that one of the vice presidents was shutting the whole place down. Robin got out of there as fast as she could.

"Merry Christmas, Betty."

She rushed past Betty's cubicle, but Betty, the god-damned dyke, was right behind her rumbling along like a green and red cement truck. On the elevator, Robin had to ride all the way down with her.

"Any plans for Christmas?" Betty asked.

"Nothing special," Robin said. Sometimes she just wanted people to leave her alone. "You know. House-mates and all. Macauley."

Mac Jenks was Robin's husband. She only called him Macauley when she had to talk with Betty Schoenfield.

"Well, you're always welcome at my place," Betty said.

"You too," Robin said. What else could she say?

When the elevator doors opened Robin was out of there like a shot. She made it past the security guard in the lobby in record time.

"Bye Robin. Merry Christmas."

"Merry Christmas," she said.

She spun through the revolving doors out onto California Street, but when she saw how mobbed the sidewalks were—Frosty the Snowman passing out cigarettes, the quartet trumpeting Jingle Bells—she took the path less traveled, meaning, in this case, Sacramento Street, which took her past the loading dock and the stoned bike messengers. One of them, who played electric bass in a band called Paula and the Pistols, wished her a merry Christmas.

"Thanks," Robin said. "Merry Christmas to you, too." She didn't remember his name.

By now Front Street was engulfed by the overflow from three saloons that had merged, like giant amoebas, in the middle of the street. Robin took a deep breath, plunged in and let herself be sucked all the way to Harrington's. She pushed through its double doors and into the mob of suits and red ties that besieged the bar—

laughing, roaring, half drunk, plastered. She got shoved up against a guy in a pinstriped suit.

"Can I buy you a drink?" he said.

"What?" Robin couldn't hear a thing.

Robin wasn't unattractive. She was almost five foot six, maybe a little too thin. Her hair was a mousey blond, but she did have admirably high cheekbones. Red-haired Sheila McCarthy always said she looked like Viva, Andy Warhol's girl, but Robin wasn't sure if that was intended as a compliment or if Sheila was just being a bitch.

"A drink?" Pinstripe shouted.

Robin dodged the question. "I'm looking for a friend, but a margarita would be nice."

"A boyfriend?" Pinstripe asked.

"A girlfriend," Robin said.

"How do you mean that, *girlfriend?*"

Pinstripe was kind of cute, and she hadn't gotten her margarita yet, but this was too good to pass up. She told him she was a lesbian

"Oh, I'm so sorry," Pinstripe said.

"For what?"

She saw good old Carl Chapman, bald and stoop shouldered, planted on a barstool right where the glossy-bright bar made a rounded turn and ran towards the back of the room. Carl was the salt of the earth, one of the supervisors in Programming but, still, he hadn't hired Robin for the trainee job she'd applied for three months before.

"Hey Robin," Carl said, as laconic and world weary as ever.

"Hey Carl. Have you seen Sheila?"

"Sheila? Back there, I think." Carl pointed down the long bar towards the sickly looking silver and blue stuffed swordfish that hung over the entrance to the kitchen. Sheila had gotten the trainee job instead of Robin.

"She's more career oriented," Carl had said.

Robin pushed towards the kitchen through suits, cigarette smoke, spilled beer, and the sickening mingle of cheap gardenia fragrances. Some asshole tried to grope her, another tried to block her way.

"Can I buy you a drink?"

When she finally found Sheila, whose red hair stood out among all the bleached blondes, Sheila stuck a huge margarita in her hand. The drink was ice cold, but it was hot and close inside the bar. When Robin took a substantial glug, the alcohol went right to her head.

"Are you okay?"

"I think so," Robin said.

But she wasn't okay. She was dizzy. Vertigo. The three piece suits, the mob at the bar, Sheila and Carl Chapman, spun past her like revolving doors. Then, she found herself floating up towards the ceiling. When the world stopped spinning, and she could look down on everything and everybody in the bar, it was wonderful. She even saw herself chatting with Sheila, drinking and smoking and having a wonderful time.

"Are you okay?" Sheila said again.

Robin was on her back flat on the floor of Harrington's, her dress wet with spilled margarita. Everyone in the place stared at her.

"I should have eaten something," she said. She started to push herself up off the floor, but Carl Chapman stopped her when she reached a sitting position.

"Just stay there a minute. Make sure you're all right. You don't have to get up."

"You've got to gain some weight," Sheila said.

"Do you have a cigarette?" Robin asked.

"You're already smoking one, honey."

#

When darkness fell in the City, the revelers began to drift away from the bars and taverns inside its financial district—going home to the wife and kids, or taking a

13

trolley bus that ground slowly up Market Street, maybe heading to the gay bars in the Castro. The lack of even a mid-winter sun caused a chill to roll over the City off the ocean. So cold that even the ice skaters, gliding along on artificial ice laid down for the season in an otherwise concrete plaza, moved towards nearby benches and removed their skates. This done, some went towards bus stops, parking lots, or the new subway whose veins coursed beneath downtown streets. Others went through the automated glass doors that opened into the huge and futuristic, stair-step atrium of the new Hyatt Regency Hotel.

As the black of night encumbered the City and its scurrying citizens, the tall buildings threw on their Christmas lights and, automatically, the City seemed to offer beauty and perhaps even hope. The lights were best seen from outside the City—on the opposite shore of the bay, or from big party boats that churned along, or even from the railing of a famed old bridge where desperate people took a last look at life.

Insignificant among the buses and cars, slowly grinding through the darkening streets, was a new 1975 Mercedes 450SL, a silver roadster with its top down despite the cold and creeping fog. A well-to-do, if aging, stockbroker that Sheila McCarthy had picked up at Harrington's drove the two women home along a route that took him through unfamiliar territory south of Market Street—wide, one-way streets that allowed Mercedes 450SL's to pass quickly through a world of shabby store fronts, empty parking lots, old residence hotels and cheap, smelly bars.

Sheila had Robin take the right hand seat where she had quickly fallen into a frozen slumber. Sheila sat half in that seat and half on the console, which allowed her to wrap her left arm around Mercedes Man's shoulders and, at the same time, hold her right hand pointing towards the curve of the car's windshield.

"Get into the right lane," she said. She bent her hand at the wrist and slowly angled it to the right as if it were an articulated bus bending at the bellows.

"Now go right," Sheila said. "Just a short block now." The bellows of her hand turned straight again. They passed a four-story residence hotel with retail shops along its length—a liquor store, a grocery, a laundromat.

"Now!" Sheila said. "Turn right!"

The first wino they encountered was the Troll. He was bearded and shriveled. He wore only a green and white t-shirt, despite the cold, and shambled along, down the middle of the street, his back to the Mercedes. He looked back over his shoulder when he heard the jolly beep of the car's German horn. He stopped, turned, and put up his fists.

"I'll knock your fucking block off, you fuckin' bastard. Right off your fucking shoulders. What-d'-ya think of that? What-d'-ya think? What-d'-ya-think of that?"

Robin woke when she heard him. He was one of the crazy ones, one of the broken down, rusted out ones, one of the ones Robin thought dangerous.

"You live *here?*" Mercedes Man said, as if he couldn't believe it.

"Oh, it's not so bad," Sheila told him. "It's kind of like living in a dark wood in a fairy tale, romantic even, don't you see?"

They arrived at the entry of an old, rundown industrial building. A sign on its solid core steel fire door read Time & Space. Electric music, hard and loud, roared inside.

"You two really live here?"

"This is the place," Sheila said. "Unusual, eh?"

"Yes. Unusual. Very."

Two winos sat on the cracked sidewalk opposite the entry with their backs against a chain link fence. Both wore Giants caps and filthy coats. Both had a three-day growth of beard. One had a classic alcoholic's, red swollen nose, the other had a crude, wood handled pocket knife in his jacket. He passed Swollen-Nose a wrinkled paper bag that held a bottle of Night Train.

"Hey man, nice car," the wino with the knife called out.

Mercedes Man tried to ignore him and flipped a switch that caused a black panel behind the seat to open. The convertible top of the Mercedes automatically rose, arching up over his head like the unwinding of a shroud.

Sheila told him, "Me and Robin and her husband live there, along with a guy from Santa Cruz. But I'm not with him or anything. And it's really cool once you get used to it. We've fixed it up, of course. We rent rehearsal space to bands."

Mercedes Man secured two latches that locked the convertible top in place. "Well, don't quit your day job."

"Hey asshole, take me for a ride in your car-car," Swollen-Nose called out.

Sheila, not knowing of the knife in the other's jacket, told Mercedes Man that the two were harmless enough.

"Would you like to come in for a minute? Have a drink or something? Some coffee?" She laughed. "And there's always live music."

"Always," Robin said with quiet sarcasm. She had wanted them to be a family, a family that cared about each other, a family that worked together and talked things out, but those things, they were not.

"I think I'd better go," Mercedes Man told Sheila. "It's Christmas Eve, you know." He turned to Robin. "I hope you feel better."

Robin told him she felt fine now. "I just fainted is all."

"Too many margaritas," Sheila told Mercedes Man, as they crawled out of his little car.

"They can do that," he said.

"Call me," Sheila said when her feet were solidly planted on the street. Mercedes Man said he would, then roared off down the alley, accelerating much too quickly.

"Well," Sheila said, "so much for that."

"Sorry," Robin told her.

"Oh hell, it doesn't matter. There's too many fish in the sea."

As the two women started towards the steel door one of the winos called out a hello. Sheila kept her head down and searched her purse for the key to the door.

"Spare change?" the dangerous one called out.

"Sorry," Robin called back. She assumed they all had knives.

three

Three days, or perhaps a week later, but certainly long after Christmas, the steel door of Time & Space opened and five unkempt young men came out of the old building. Four were rockers, Asian-American bluesmen, members of Bobby Sun and Blues Dragon. Three of them turned right towards Fifth Street, but the band's leader, Bobby Sun, and Robin's husband, Mac Jenks, turned left towards Sixth.

A Filipino wino with hooks for hands staggered towards them asking for spare change.

"Spare change? I haven't eaten all day."

Mac pointed up Natoma. "Go up to Jimmy Huang's Mission," he said. "He'll feed you."

Mac was stocky but athletic. Black stubble grew from his cheeks and chin because he avoided shaving whenever he could. Mac was afraid of gashing his fingers, his hand, maybe even his throat, whenever he slipped an old blade out of his decrepit, old Gillette razor. He knew his fear was unreasonable, maybe even certifiable, but still he refused to buy an electric. His face never felt truly clean when he used electrics.

Bobby Sun, who fronted the band, had long, black hair tied in a horsetail. He had pierced ears set off with silver studs. He wore wrap-around dark glasses because he had seen what the evil eye could do. He carried two long, thin guitar cases that held his Strat and his old Epiphone.

He asked Mac how the band had sounded.

"A little flat," Mac told him. Once, Mac Jenks had played electric bass in a little band four army surgeons had started. They'd entertained in officer's clubs, in the wards of the wounded and, once, on the hospital ship Repose on station in the South China Sea. A bass was what held a band together but, even so, the surgeons, being officers, had made him stand behind them.

"I didn't think we had any energy today," Bobby Sun said. "You know what I'm sayin'?"

"It didn't sound bad," Mac said without emotion. "It sounded okay."

"Okay?" Bobby Sun shook his head but kept his eyes on the gray sidewalk. "The band has gotta be tight, man. Not just okay. Like, you know, if we're really gonna make it. Tight." Bobby's band had a gig at a punk club on Broadway set for a Tuesday night in February.

"It's energy, man," Bobby Sun said. "You know? It's all about energy. You know what I'm sayin'?"

"Yeah," Mac said. "I know. Sometimes it's just hard to get it up."

Mac had a five-year lease on the old building on Natoma. He'd gotten it cheap, because it was as rundown as he was. For now, at least, he rented out the first floor as practice space for bands—Crime, The Nuns, and other local bands more avant-garde than Bobby Sun's. Taj Mahal and his Hula Blues Band had practiced there once, even Sly and the Family Stone. Mac called the business "Time & Space" because that was what the bands rented, time and space.

"What's up with Robin, man?" Bobby Sun said. "Out of body or something, up to the ceiling. Like some kind of New Age shit?" Bobby's old, toothless Ford was parked up on the sidewalk in front of a battered green dumpster.

Mac shrugged his rounding shoulders. "The tequila just went to her head too fast." He cracked a one liner, "Even pigs can fly when they drink tequila."

"It sounded to me more like a vision or something. You know, seeing herself down below and all." Bobby Sun unlocked the door of the beat-to-shit Ford then turned back to Mac and thanked him for fronting him some money and rehearsal time.

"You'll come out ahead on this," Bobby said. "I guarantee it."

Mac Jenks trusted Bobby Sun. Mac had seen the rotten heart of humanity—3rd Field Hospital, 811th Medical Group, Saigon. Bobby had seen it, too—205th Assault Helicopter Company, based in the Iron Triangle. Bobby had been a door gunner, a stone cold killer pissing his pants.

Bobby slipped the key into the ignition and cranked the engine. The Ford kicked over but stalled out. Bobby turned the ignition off then tried again. When the car finally started, Bobby Sun gunned the engine until it ran smooth—smoother at any rate. Not too much sputter.

"I gotta get a new car," Bobby said. "Gotta get me some bread."

"I hear that." Prices were going up like crazy—gasoline, food, cigarettes. Even cheap red wine wasn't so cheap anymore. Mac gave a wave of his hand to Bobby Sun as Bobby pulled away from the dumpster and accelerated way too fast down the narrow alley.

A train wreck, unshaven Mac Jenks thought. All of it, a train wreck.

At the very beginning, when they'd first moved into Time & Space—Mac and Robin, Sheila McCarthy and an insurance underwriter nee beach bum named Joey Wooten—the building was naked concrete and empty. It was filthy dirty, as musty as a tomb and littered with old newspapers, beer cans, scraps of wood and cardboard.

In its previous life the building had been a print shop—textbooks, shopping news, signs, letterheads, odd jobs. Then, it had held big presses and small presses, four-color presses and surrounding those had been a regiment of stitchers, joggers and plate makers. Above all that, on the second floor, had been systemized stocks of ink and chemical solvents, reams of paper in cardboard boxes. Half of the third floor had been a lunchroom for employees, complete with tables, chairs, restrooms and a kitchen.

Mac, and the others, had trapped the mice in the kitchen in humane traps and released them in the little park on Sixth Street. But this compassionate act had upset the balance of nature and the cockroaches had taken over the kitchen. They added a table in the center of it where they ate their meals, and a tabletop toaster oven where they cooked them. The industrial strength bathroom had two showers, three toilets, three sinks, and two urinals. They'd painted it boring beige because beige paint had been on sale at a Mission District store. They'd put up medicine cabinets and a big mirror they got cheap at Goodwill because it was cracked along the diagonal and reflected perverse images of everything. They divided the lunchroom off into three narrow bedrooms. They'd turned the huge open space that made up the rest of the third floor into a living room—three sofas from Goodwill, a thin orange carpet that was already curling up around the edges, and a brand new, aluminum ping-pong table.

In the rehearsal space on the first floor they'd nailed together a wooden platform a foot off the concrete floor so the emerging musicians they rented to could perch on it as if it were a stage. They'd glued a whole shit-load of egg cartons—big thirty-six egg, egg trays—onto the bare concrete walls, trying to keep the electric music on the first floor from fibrillating their hearts on the second and third.

Now, on the little stage, Mac negotiated with a punked-out band called Roily Bitches. Their leader was a skin and bones white woman—tight black leggings, Sex Pistols t-shirt, hair done up in a green, three inch high mohawk. She had gold stars in her nose and cheeks but no money.

"Next week. I promise," she told Mac. "The whole thing. Well, most of it maybe."

"I'll have to switch your schedule otherwise," Mac said. "You know, it's like everybody wants Saturday morning."

"But that's our time," Mohawk Girl said.

"No, its my time. You guys are just renting it."

Mac escaped toward the concrete stairs just as Mohawk Girl gave the band a down beat: "One, two, one, two, three, four ..." Roily Bitches expelled an electric thud that hit him in the back like a kidney punch. The steps were wide but low. Mac took them two at a time to get away from Roily Bitches' loud angry song.

"You slit your wrist you stupid bitch ..."

He slowed at the turn on the second floor landing—a trip and fall here could prove fatal. An empty freight elevator shaft plunged downwards, all the way to a basement of bare concrete, dripping pipes and airless odors. The printing business' creditors had taken out the elevator car, its mechanisms, and even the gates that guarded the shaft. Mac had nailed up a big "X" made of one by fours across the openings on each floor and tacked a red flag dead center on each "X."

When Mac and the others were almost done with their "remodeling" work and were punchy from days and days of cleaning, nailing up sheetrock, painting and plastering, they'd used the empty shaftway as a dumpster. They tossed shards of sheetrock, bits of plywood and empty plastic buckets down it. Red-haired Sheila McCarthy had gone so far as to drop an old TV down the shaft, and they laughed like lunatics when it shattered.

Now, still pursued by Roily Bitches' suffocating music, Mac escaped the twisted stairs, into the endless emptiness of the unrestored second floor. There the feedback Roily Bitches produced blended with the pop pop pop of Mac's little Colt .22LR revolver. It was Saturday, and Sheila, who had finally finished setting up her darkroom, had taken the black Colt from Mac's old, metal desk. She was squeezing off rounds aimed at a target that stood in front of the foot thick concrete wall.

Mac had found an article in Popular Mechanics showing how to build an indoor gun range step-by-step—railroad ties and a ton of dirt for starters. All that was impossible, so Mac faked it. He'd filled cardboard boxes with what remained of the egg flats, nail-gunned sheetrock to the wall, and figured it would do. After all, the gunmetal Colt was only a twenty-two.

Sheila pretended to quick draw, pulling the pistol from the waistband of her jeans. She sent a bee-sized slug sizzling towards the target. The egg flats didn't stop it so it smacked into the sheetrock and then the concrete. Mac mimed escaping a ricocheting bullet. He raised his arms slowly as if to protect his face. He bent backwards at the waist turning his head to watch an imaginary bullet pass right by his nose, then another and another. He fell in a tumbling, twisting, ludicrous way—Buster Keaton, Charles Chaplin, Harold Lloyd.

Sheila laughed, but when Mac didn't get up immediately, she asked him if he was all right.

"Yeah," he said as he pushed himself up, off the concrete floor. "But I'm way out of practice. That really hurt."

He'd tried doing stand-up comedy in L.A. before he'd married Robin. One club manager told him that he liked the pratfalls, but that his monologue, about playing bass guitar in Vietnam, made audiences uncomfortable.

Mac took the empty revolver from Sheila and carelessly pushed its business end up against her third eye, right in the middle of her forehead.

"No more quick draw, Red. Got that? Don't John Wayne your gun."

She pushed the revolver away, took his cheeks between her hands and kissed him, like Bugs Bunny would, wet and sloppy, on the lips. "Don't you reckon I'm man enough, *podner*?"

four

Monday morning in the City. In Bernal Heights, in the Richmond, the Castro, in Noe Valley, alarm clocks buzzed like electroshock. On Potrero Hill, Russian Hill, Telegraph Hill, in Chinatown, the Panhandle, the Mission, dreamers hit the snooze, drifted until the second shock then hit the ground running. Toilets flushed. Showers sprayed. All across the City age old iron pipes shuddered and the water pressure dropped.

"Goddamn it!"

No time for breakfast. Just coffee. Grab a donut. Sugar rush. Platform Shoes. Caffeine rush. White shirts.

Neckties—"Oh God how I hate these things."

Panty hose—"Oh God how I hate these things."

Downtown. Market Street. The rain poured down in buckets. Cars and buses tangled. The pace of life tried to quicken but snarl was pandemic. Trolley buses, diesel buses, taxi cabs all unable to move.

"You're late! You're late! For an unimportant date."

Tall buildings began to fill. Elevators transmogrified into sardine cans.

"Watch it, mister. Jesus!"

Automobiles swooped down off the gray bridge that spanned the bay. Exhaust choked the air. Cars clunked over the thick, iron plates that covered holes dug in the street. At Market and Van Ness, traffic signals went crazy and blinked green then red then green again. South of Market a thousand parking lots filled with a million cars. Corner bars began to open: the Pastime, the Dew-Drop-Inn, the Sports-Para-Dice. Cold Beer, No Loitering. Pawn-shop owners raised the clanking steel cages that protected their windows. Doors were unlocked. Safes were opened. Cash drawers were shoved into registers.

At Sixth and Howard the day of the week didn't matter much. Winos who huddled in doorways began to unfold their rain-stiff bodies. Junkies with green, infected veins crawled out of the pastel colored conduits the City had setup in the little park of grass and concrete paths. Homeless, foodless, hopeless men began to line up in front of SOMA Mission, waiting impatiently for Pastor Jimmy Huang's morning offering.

"Spare change?"

"Got a cigarette?"

"I bring a message of hope."

#

Robin slapped the snooze bar on her clock radio with her long right hand, and the buzzing stopped. Sleep clouded her eyes. The buzzing started again. Slap. Buzz. Buzz. Buzz. She fumbled for her cigarettes. She took her first drag. She coughed, but her heart started thumping again. Mac was asleep beside her. The bastard hadn't budged an inch. She looked at the clock radio and realized how late she was.

"Shit."

Robin sat on the edge of the bed, lit another cigarette and tried to remember the flying dream she'd had. But when she took another drag, the dream ran away from her—the harder she tried to catch it, the faster it ran. She slipped a rose colored bathrobe over her flannel nightgown and stumbled, barefoot, out the bedroom door and down the long hallway to a kitchen of dirty dishes and scurrying cockroaches. She found a cup that was almost clean among the pile of plates in the sink and rinsed it out. She filled it with water as warm as the tap could get it then stirred in instant coffee and milk.

She had met Mac five years before all this—before Time & Space, before booming bands, winos and skid row. She had finally gotten out of Glendale and away from her mother and railroad tracks. She had her own little place in San Bernardino nearer to mountains and trees and lakes. She had a good job at Wells Fargo, and she'd even bought a car. Then one day Mac walked into her bank, came up to her window to cash a check drawn on a Wells Fargo in Hollywood. He was just out of the army, then, and looked ever so fit and handsome. They had coffee. He was trying to make it as a stand-up comic but, like so many others, he'd discovered that Hollywood's starry sidewalks had become the haunt of run away kids, street people, hustlers and junkies.

Now, Robin rushed into the industrial strength bathroom sloshing coffee all over the floor. There were two urinals, two showers and a full-length mirror on a stand that she and Sheila had insisted on having. Robin stopped at one of the sinks. It faced the long, warped mirror with the crack that zigzagged down the middle. She put two hands on the sink for support and closed her cloudy eyes for just a moment. She opened the medicine cabinet that she and Mac shared and pulled out her dental floss. Her grandfather had false teeth that he'd put in a dish every night on the bedside table. Sometimes he'd forget to put them back in. Robin flossed three times a day. A piece of floss broke off and stuck between Robin's teeth.

"Shit!" She dug at it with a fingernail.

The toothpaste tube was completely flat and completely empty, but she managed to squeeze a dab onto her
toothbrush and started brushing her teeth. As always,
she could see two of herself inside the warped mirror,
slightly offset, almost as if she were standing beside
herself.

"Mirror, mirror on the wall ..." she said.

She spit a load of toothpaste into the sink. When
she looked up again another woman's face was beside
her's in the mirror. The woman looked so much like Robin
that, at first, she thought the cracked mirror was playing
tricks again. The woman had dishwater blond hair, a
slender face, high cheekbones, but the face was older
than Robin's, even haggard. She said hello, but the
woman didn't answer. She bent down to spit again, and
when she looked up again the woman, the reflection, was
gone.

Sheila McCarthy slipped into the bathroom already
dressed and ready to go—pants suit, comfy flats, hair
done up. Skinny Robin had always envied her handsome
breasts and gentle curves.

"Jesus," Sheila said. "I thought I was late, but look
at you."

Robin spat into the sink. "Your new girlfriend was
in here a minute ago," she said. Sheila was a switch
hitter.

"My new girlfriend? I don't have a new girlfriend.
Got a cigarette? I've got enough trouble with the old
girlfriends."

Robin dug into the pocket of her bathrobe for her
cigarettes.

"It must have been Joey's," she said, "new girlfriend, that is." She lit Sheila's cigarette with a flick of her
Bic. "Whatever happened to quitting?"

Sheila looked at herself in the full-length mirror,
turning left then right. "Me quit? Fat chance ... Joey's got

a new girlfriend? I thought he was all hung up on what's-her-name, the Jew."

"Well yes, but you know how fast things can change these days."

"Gotta fly," Sheila said. "It's raining out you know."

Robin took a quick shower that went from warm to cold because the water heater was a piece of junk. While she dried off she scolded herself for letting Sheila run off with her cigarettes. She had to assert herself more. It was just like her goddamn boss making her wait on Christmas Eve for some goddamn nonexistent letter. Still damp, she dashed back to the bedroom.

There wasn't much to it: a king sized bed that filled most of the room, a wardrobe that was way too small, an old wooden rocker where Robin threw her clothes, a lamp, bedside table, a clock radio and Mac.

He was just stirring. He sat on the edge of the bed in blue and red striped boxer shorts. He coughed and asked Robin for a cigarette. She told him she was out, even though she still had a whole pack hidden in her purse. Mac searched out the longest butt he could find in an ashtray that lay on the floor, dusted it off and lit up. He pointed at the clock radio and told Robin she was running late.

"Way, way late."

"Like I didn't know." Robin pulled on her goddamn pantyhose, and asked Mac if he had a hangover.

"What do you think?" Mac said. They had gone to a new comedy club the night before. They'd laughed and drunk, then laughed and drunk some more. Mac talked nonstop about a new routine he was working on that had slapstick in it.

"You know, Buster Keaton. Charlie Chaplin."

Robin had a hangover too.

She got dressed as fast as she could then went back to the bathroom, looked at herself in the full length mirror and thought she looked passable at least. She dashed back to the kitchen and pulled a Hershey bar out of a big, mouse proof pickle jar. Umbrella in one hand, handbag slung over her shoulder, she unwrapped the Hershey bar as she quickstepped through the living room.

There, a stray cat Sheila had taken in sharpened its claws on a Goodwill easy chair.

"Scat!"

Robin went flying down the concrete stairs, double time, eating the candy bar. It was like the unwinding of a dream. Second floor: Sheila's darkroom, Mac's metal desk, tons of empty space. First floor: empty rehearsal space, sixteen gauge, steel door. She had to pull hard to open it, and when it opened the rain depressed her all the more. It splashed down hard. The wind blowing up a gale. She raised her umbrella, but it was so old the latch was weak and the wind pressed it right back down on her arm.

"Shit."

She fumbled with the goddamn thing and dropped her goddamn candy bar. The rushing rainwater propelled it down the gutter.

"Shit."

She thought about picking it up, but she never ate very much, anyway.

five

That night, Robin made dinner—beans and franks, a small salad, day old white cake. She served it on a table that stood dead center in the cockroach-infested kitchen. The table was a remnant of the building's past life as a print shop. It was a stout brute with thick wooden legs and a sheet metal surface that had once supported a paper jogger that handled 28" by 28" pages.

Sheila was out surfing the fern bars on Union Street that night so there were only three members of Robin's fragile, little family at the heavy table. When Robin laid Mac's plate in front of him he slid his left arm across the tin tabletop and snapped up a blood red bottle of ketchup. Mac put ketchup on everything—franks and beans, liver and onions, corned beef hash, eggs, pot roast, baked potatoes. He pulled the bottle towards him and gave it several shakes.

When the ketchup didn't flow, he inverted the bottle until it was perpendicular to his plate, and tapped the neck of the bottle three taps with his fingers. When the ketchup still didn't flow, he sat straight up in his chair—for more leverage Robin thought—and held the bottle at an angle to his plate. Every time he hit the bottom of the poor bottle with the heel of his hand Robin tried not to wince. She turned toward Joey Wooten, to distract herself, and asked him if he had a new girlfriend.

"Not to my knowledge," replied Joey. His blond hair was all that was left of his beach days—swimming, surfing, beach volleyball. The whole nine yards. He just couldn't do it anymore, that was all.

"You're sure you didn't have a woman in here last night?"

"I wasn't that drunk."

"Yes you were," Mac Jenks said, crunching down salad, slapping the bottom of the ketchup bottle.

#

Later, Robin and Joey pushed two "liberated" shopping carts full of dirty laundry out of Time & Space's steel doorway and into the world of the Natoma—too narrow to be called a street, too wide to be called an alley. At night it became more dangerous, like most of the City's haunts. There were streetlights, yes, but they were too dim and too far apart, so the shadows on the sidewalks became dark lairs where monsters might lurk. Winos who'd failed to find lodging in Pastor Jimmy Huang's dormitory, and had no money for even the cheapest residence hotels, tended to avoid Natoma at night, preferring the brighter lights and broader sidewalks of Howard Street. Those who remained stayed hunkered down in doorways drinking fortified wine mixed with lighter fluid until it left them insensate and at last unconscious.

The rain had stopped. The gutters no longer ran with water, but the street was still wet. The two winos in Giants caps—the one with the swollen red nose and the one who carried the cheap folding knife—sat cross-legged, leaning their backs against the chain link fence across from Time & Space.

"Hey, faggot, wash my socks, eh?" Swollen-Nose called.

Joey Wooten kept on walking, short steps as if he were hobbled.

"Hey faggot! Is that why you walk so dumb?"

Joey tried to ignore him. His gait was unsteady because his left foot had been crushed in a car accident down in Monterey. Even after three surgeries he had to wear a brace to keep from dragging the foot. Drop foot, they called it, and because of it he'd left the sweet sun, the surf, and the soft, volleyball sand behind.

The wino with the knife tried to stand but lost his footing on the wet sidewalk and fell back against the fence.

Swollen-Nose called to Robin. "Hey sweetheart. Give me a hundred thousand so I can buy a bar."

The other, as unhinged as the first, found his play-mate's question hysterical. "You can't buy a bar for a lousy hundred thousand, you fuckin' drunk."

"Make it two hundred," Swollen-Nose said.

Robin just kept walking.

Joey's shopping cart had a bad wheel that clattered as he pushed it over the sidewalk's edge, onto the wet, shimmering asphalt. Walking up the center of the street was sometimes safer than staying on Natoma's shadowed sidewalks. But the Troll that guarded the entrance to the street challenged him to a fight.

"I'll knock your fucking block off, you fuckin' fag. Right off your fucking shoulders. Right into the goddamn fucking gutter. What-d'-ya think of that. What-d'-ya think?"

A voice came out from under the Goodwill loading dock. "Shut your fuckin' mouth Charlie, I'm trying to sleep for Chrissakes."

On the right hand corner of the intersection at Sixth and Natoma there was a friendly little grocery store owned by a turbaned Sikh called Livpreet Singh. The door was always open and inviting, but still, Livpreet kept a loaded, semi-automatic Glock 17 just under the counter below the cash register.

But Joey and Robin didn't stop to buy cigarettes, wine, or even ice cream as they frequently did. Instead they turned their shopping carts full of dirty clothes to the left, down Sixth Street towards the Sixth Street Coin Operated Laundry. Joey stepped ahead of Robin, and when they arrived, he opened the heavy glass door of the Coin Op. Inside a black man with a purple Afro drank from a bottle in a brown paper bag and a half-sane bag lady, dozed against a paint-peeled wall. A muscle bound white man called Harpo because of his thick curly hair sat behind the counter near the door watching a black and white television. His job was to eject anyone who wasn't actually doing laundry and beat the shit out of any wino that tried to urinate in the doorway.

He looked up from the TV. "Robin," he said, "Joey."

Each of them answered in turn. "Hi Harpo." "Hi, Harpo."

Harpo turned back toward the television and adjusted the rabbit ears, "Monday Night at the Movies."

After Joey and Robin shoveled Time & Space's dirty laundry into five front loaders, added detergent and selected water temperatures, they inserted their quarters and pushed various buttons. When the machines started churning they sat down next to each other on two of the old vinyl chairs that lined the walls. Robin opened her handbag and pulled out a paperback book. Joey snuck a peek—*Transcendental Meditation*. He wasn't interested in that so he turned his attention to the tangled dance of soapy suds and dirty laundry in the glass doors of the washers. The laundromat's tumbling foam was about as close as he ever got to the ocean these days.

The bag lady, awake now, waddled over to them, holding a hard-boiled egg between the thumb and forefinger of her right hand. "Got any mayonnaise?" she asked.

Robin said, "I think I might." She shoveled through her shoulder bag. "Here." She gave a small foil packet to the bag lady.

"Good," the bag lady said.

"Good," Robin replied

Joey remembered Robin's question about girl-friends from dinner and, the more he thought about it, the more curious it seemed. He leaned towards her and playfully bumped her left shoulder with his right. She ignored him at first, but he bumped her hard, then harder again, and finally pressed his shoulder so hard against her that she had to bend sideways.

She started laughing but stopped herself. "Come on, Joey. I'm trying to read."

"Why did you ask me if I had a new girlfriend?"

She looked up from her book. "Oh, no reason."

"You must have had a reason," Joey said.

There were two, little, rumpled paper bags inside Robin's four dimensional shoulder bag, and inside each of those was a twenty-four ounce can of Colt 45 Malt Liquor. She took one out and showed it to Joey.

"Want some?"

With the can still in its paper bag, the two of them both coughed to disguise the ripping of the aluminum tab and the hissing of pressures equalizing. Harpo, at the front counter, glanced over his right shoulder in the direction of the cough, the rip, and the hiss then went back to his movie.

Robin passed the open can to Joey. He put his mouth around the tin-cold opening of the pull-top and guzzled.

"Hey! Leave some for me," Robin said.

They passed the can back and forth for a while, exchanging glugs of the Colt 45. When it was almost gone Robin became talkative. "I'll tell you why, if you promise not to tell anyone, and especially not Mac."

Joey Wooten promised. "Sure. No problem," he said. "I promise." Most of the time Joey kept his promises.

She reconstructed her morning for him: oversleeping, instant coffee, cold shower, industrial strength bathroom, dental floss. She told him about brushing her teeth, and of how a woman appeared behind her in the warped mirror that spanned the sinks.

"At first I thought it was one of Sheila's girlfriends ..."

"She does go through them fast," Joey said.

A tall, skinny black man walked into the laundry. Harpo put his arm out like the gate at a railroad crossing and stopped him at the door.

"You got laundry to do?"

"You got to let me in, man. It's important. I got to talk with Joey." He was so shaky that Robin mistook him for a junky.

"No, he's okay," Joey told her. He called out to Harpo, "He's okay," and Harpo, assenting, let the black man in.

Walking back to where Joey was, the man's trembling grew so much worse. He seemed to be coming unglued, and Joey invited him to take a seat.

"Jesus man, Jesus. You've got to help me out, man. You've got to."

When he wasn't so agitated, Joey introduced him to Robin as Clarence Davis. "He has a room in the Majestic."

"Oh, that Clarence," she said.

"Its the ants, man. You know what I'm sayin'? All just scurrying around. I broke my ant farm. It fell and cracked, and now they're all lost and scurrying around. We got to find 'em and patch it up and put them back in before the manager comes and kills 'em."

Joey dug into the front pocket of his jeans and fished out two dollars and change. He gave it to Clarence and told him to walk up to Mission Street and get himself a burrito.

"Eat something, Clarence. If you spend it on wine I won't help you. Have a burrito, and then go home. We'll be finished with the laundry by then, and I'll come by and help you."

Later that night, Robin walked in her sleep for the first time in years.

six

George Zumpo's cousins in Markleeville had given him the names of more cousins all around the Bay. He rang many doorbells and even tapped on some windows, but none of his so-called cousins would tell him anything about Leela.

"How would I know anything about Leela?"

"I haven't seen Leela in years."

His cousin Willie Stokes told him he looked like a goddamned bum. "You make all Indians look bad."

Zumpo had heard that one before, but when cousin Willie threatened to call the police Zumpo fled for his life.

But in the City, at SOMA Mission, he happened to meet a crazy woman who told him about a Road Chief who lived in a big old house on 17th Street hill that was painted blue and grey and had a hundred steps leading up to the front door. Zumpo found that house and climbed those steps. There wasn't an electric doorbell with a button to push, but an old time, manual twist doorbell that sounded a bell when Zumpo turned it.

The chief's name was Eddie Birdsong, and he welcomed Zumpo instead of throwing him out. He gave Zumpo mescal, and Zumpo told him he was seeking his wife, his white German Shepherd, and his Volkswagen Westfalia camper, but not necessarily in that order.

Chief Birdsong told him that Leela was going to nursing school at a place called U.C.S.F., but that he knew nothing of the dog or camper.

The next day Zumpo, the great walker, crawled out from under the Goodwill loading dock and climbed up and over the famous hills of the City. He found them like mole hills compared to the mountains of the high Sierras. There were no cable cars, either. He saw no flower children. He saw no Chinatowns. And where was Karl Malden and, for that matter, Michael Douglas?

After much wandering and questioning of passersby he at last found the nursing school and went in to make inquiries. After he got thrown out, he sat on the brick front steps and waited. And waited. At last, he decided that rather than waste more time sitting down and smelling the roses, he should try to make a living.

"Spare change? Got any spare change?" Zumpo collected three dollars and thirty-five cents, two half eaten bags of chips, and a partially filled can of Coca-Cola, but none of Dr. Pepper, which was his favorite.

The next day Zumpo walked to the nursing school again, and a man in a white shirt and red tie came out of the building and accosted him. The man gave Zumpo a dollar and told him to leave. On the third day, the same man came out and gave him a tuna sandwich on a French roll wrapped in plastic and told him that if he sat there any longer the police would be called.

"I'm sorry," the man told him. "But we just can't have this."

"I won't do it anymore," Zumpo promised.

That was why, on the fourth day, Zumpo did not sit on the brick steps but on the curb of a loading zone with his legs stretched out over a fishless stream that ran along the gutter.

"Spare change?" Zumpo was a fisher of money.

seven

Another morning. Robin was late again. Pee. Luke-warm coffee. Toothbrush. No woman in the cracked mirror. Cold shower. Hershey bar. Down the stairs. Bobby Sun and Blues Dragon blasted out the blues—"If you see my little red rooster ..." Out the steel door. She locked it.

Robin made a right, turned her head into the wind and dashed up Natoma. The Troll sat huddled up by a forest green dumpster. When he saw her, he stumbled to his feet and put up his fists.

"So when the motherfucker come up to me I hit the bastard. What-d'-ya think of that? What-d'-ya think?"

What else can desperate people do, Robin thought, but drink fortified wine?

When she stepped off the curb a blue and yellow Chronicle delivery van doing about sixty, blasted its horn. She pulled back just in time, and then she realized, she'd missed a splendid chance to do herself in. When the van swung left, into the Chronicle lot, Robin swung right and started walking again. When she got to Fifth Street she saw an army of business suits trekking north from the bus stops and parking lots south of Market—marching feet, honking horns, roaring buses. Carbon monoxide.

She paused, looked for an opening, and then merged into the heart of the march. Heads down, no one speaking. Past Minna Street. Past the Old Mint. Past Mission. Towards Market Street and the revolving doors of big buildings.

Robin usually walked all the way to work to save money, but this time she was really, really late. There was a trolley bus stopped right at Market and Fifth, and the driver waited with the door open while she made a run for it.

"Thanks," she said.

"No problem."

She balanced against the round, steel hand railing by the farebox and dug through her purse. Exact change only. Since the bus was nearing the end of the line, there was an empty seat right up front, and Robin took it. She swallowed a deep breath of poisoned air and, falling asleep, dreamed herself a white gull circling, floating on air, high above the City.

The gull's thermal vision, being infrared, made the bay waters appear turquoise, the big buildings blue, the streets and sidewalks lavender. To the gull, high above Sixth Street, the damaged men in front of Jimmy Huang's became monstrous caricatures in violet, red and black. Just around the corner, gliding down Natoma alley, catching an updraft, the gull saw the same haunting things that Robin saw everyday—winos urinating honey against the broken walls of grim black buildings.

#

10:15 a.m. Coffee break.

On the twenty-second floor of the Consolidated Bank Building the young women of the Word Processing Department grabbed their company issued coffee mugs and headed for the coffee room. Robin Jenks was in the midst of them, mug in hand.

Everyone in the whole goddamn company, from the president on down to Robin, had been issued an ugly, white coffee mug, and told to take good care of it because they wouldn't get another. Robin had typed the memo herself. The next day the disposable Styrofoam cups in the coffee room disappeared. A nickel here, a nickel there.

As Robin waited for an elevator, she waved at Jackie, the receptionist, in the company's twenty-second floor lobby.

"Don't worry, I'll be right back," Robin said.

Jackie wore a telephone headset. "Good morning, Consolidated Bankers." Jackie had skin the color of coffee and cream, and salesmen always remarked on how beautiful she was. Robin figured that was why she'd got the job—a beautiful, highly visible, token black.

Up in the elevator. Twenty-third floor. Customer Service. Accounting. Coffee room.

"Hey Sheila."

"Hey Robin. Did you make it into work on time?"

"What do you think?"

Robin got in line at the coffee urn behind Amy Balaba, a wasp-waisted Filipino woman whose taste in colors ran to combinations of purple and pink.

"Are you okay?" she asked Robin. "I heard that you've been sleepwalking."

They knew about it. Goddamn Sheila, the gossipy bitch. "I'm fine, yes," Robin told Amy Balaba. "I sleepwalked as a kid you know. Lots of kids do. I hadn't done it since, until now, that is."

"And Sheila saved you?" Amy stepped up to the urn and filled her company issued mug without even having to look at what she was doing.

"Not exactly, I was just standing in front of the refrigerator eating cake. I didn't need any rescuing."

"What do you see sleepwalking? Can you see spirits and such things like that?"

"I don't think so. No, I mean. I don't ever remember anything at all."

"You be careful then."

Robin managed a smile. "Don't worry I will."

Everyone in the goddamned coffee room looked like they bought their clothing at Sears—tasteless floral patterns, cheap pants suits, knee high boots, platform shoes. Pudgy women in loose black dresses that made them look even fatter and all of them knew about her sleepwalking now. They glanced up from their sugar donuts as if she were on exhibit in a zoo then looked away the minute her eyes caught theirs. She wished everyone would just leave her alone.

She got her coffee as fast as she could and dashed for the elevators. When one finally stopped and the doors opened on twenty-three one of the executives from thirty stepped out and she almost crashed into him—with coffee in hand no less.

"Oh, sorry." He barely even looked at her. She hated elevators, hated narrow places, closets, hallways, alleys, even the thought of caskets made her squeamish. It was one thing she and Mac had in common, but she wasn't sure if that was good or bad.

Jackie the receptionist was already halfway out of her telephone headset when Robin stepped out into the twenty-second floor lobby. "I sure am glad to see you." Jackie dashed off so quickly Robin figured she had to pee.

Robin sat down, slipped on the headset, and answered a call. "Good morning, Consolidated Bankers."

When she finally had a free minute she got Sheila, the bitch, on the line. "Shall we have lunch?" she asked, sweet as could be.

"Usual place?" Sheila asked.

"Usual place," Robin told her.

At noon, she met red-haired Sheila McCarthy in a little sandwich shop on Front Street. It was packed full of people like always, and buzzing with so much chatter Robin could barely hear her own thoughts as they ran through her head. In line at the steam table she got her usual turkey on Russian rye but with coleslaw instead of potato salad. She got two little screw cap bottles of red wine, too. Hair of the dog. Sheila could get away with leaving early for lunch and had saved a seat for her. When Robin sat down she gave Sheila one of the little bottles of wine.

"Oh thanks, how sweet of you."

She started to tell Sheila off for spreading rumors. But before she could even get going, Sheila started bitching about some guy she'd met at a party.

"What a prick," Sheila said. "He got his goddamn sex and then he just left. I mean, like, he could've at least have had some coffee or something."

Robin tried to ignore all that and tried to explain how tired she was. Sheila put her hand on top of Robin's as it rested on the varnished tabletop.

"Well, you've got to get your rest, honey. I mean you are burning the candle at both ends."

"Not that kind of tired. Well, that kind of tired, too, but ..."

"I had a roommate in college who was a sleep-walker," Sheila said. "Sometimes I'd come home from a date. Real late, you know? And she'd be standing by the window or something. Awake but not really awake. Like in a dream world."

"Whatever happened to her?"

"I don't know. She flunked out, I think." Sheila pointed at the long, green slice of pickle that lay untouched on Robin's plate. "Don't you want it?"

eight

On the fifth day of Zumpo's vigil at the nursing school, Leela finally came out of the old iron doors. She was in a nurse's uniform that was half covered by a heavy fringe jacket Zumpo had once liberated from a western outfitters store—a simple matter of prestidigitation. Leela had a heavy tote bag over her left shoulder filled with more books than Zumpo had read in his entire life. He always knew she was smart but not that smart.

He stood up and tipped his big, black Stetson with the eagle feather in the hat band.

Leela gave him a warning. "Georgie! You can't sit here anymore. They're going to call the cops if you sit here anymore."

Zumpo assumed his most innocent, and even righteous, posture. "But I'm not sitting anywhere."

"You know what I mean, Georgie. Don't give me any bullshit."

He offered her some cheese puffs from a bag of Cheetos some rich white girl had thrown into the garbage can by the steps. Zumpo thought his gesture to be very nice, even sweet in fact but, still, she wouldn't cut him any slack.

"Please leave me alone, Georgie. I don't love you anymore. I really don't."

"Hah!" he said. "Then why did you come out to warn me against the cops?"

"If the cops get you, the cops get you. But it's five o'clock, and Mike is coming to pick me up. He's awfully mad at you, you know."

"I don't have anything against Mike. Why is Mike mad at me?" Mike Weasel's only sin was that he was the brother of Charlie Weasel who was the very weasel who'd lured Leela away from Zumpo while he was locked up in jail in Gardnerville.

"Why doesn't Charlie come himself?" He had her dead to rights. "If you were still my woman, I'd come to pick you up personally. I'm the one who loves you."

"You don't really love me, Georgie. You just want me because you can't have me. That's all. When you had me, you didn't want me, did you?"

"Of course I did," Zumpo said. Zumpo didn't think it was a matter of "you don't miss your water 'til the well runs dry." But his well had run dry and he did miss her. He lit a cigarette so he could think, and that was when Mike Weasel drove up in Zumpo's 1965 Volkswagen Westfalia camper.

Mike looked the same as always: pock marked face, skinny, greasy-haired and just plain ugly. He rolled down the driver's side window. "Hey, queer bait! Get away from my sister!"

"She ain't your sister, she's my wife. And what the fuck are you doing driving my camper?"

Leela stepped between Zumpo and the van. "You go to hell, Georgie. It's my van. I paid for it, remember."

"Community property," Zumpo told her. "I want you. I want my Westfalia camper, and I want White Dog."

Leela pulled her heavy tote bag up higher on her shoulder. "I gotta go, Georgie. But this is the last time, okay? Don't come here anymore. Next time, cops."

"Go away, man," Mike shouted. "Don't you know when you're not wanted?"

On his way back to Natoma and his place under the Goodwill loading dock, Zumpo, the great walker, saw many curious sights like the gray, concrete housing projects where the black people lived. For a while he pretended that the sick, skinny trees spaced out along the sidewalk were the tall pines of the Sierra, and that the delivery vans, the Yellow Cabs, and fuming cars, were light footed deer and heavyset bears. In Sagetown there'd been jackrabbits, rattlesnakes, coyotes, and winos. He'd fished many times for catfish in Mud Lake and for trout in the West Carson. But he'd only hunted once, and that was when he was a kid and hadn't known that he did not like the killing. The truth was that he'd never seen a bear in his life, and most of the deer he'd seen had been those at the edges of highways who'd been murdered by motorists.

It was true that he wanted Leela and also true that he couldn't have her. Yes, but that was not why he loved her. He had always loved her, ever since the first time he'd seen her in a white man's school in Gardnerville.

On Hayes Street he saw a bus shelter where a crippled man with a cane sat and waited. Further along, he saw a black woman who wore tennis shoes but no socks pushing a shopping cart full of aluminum cans. He saw a locksmith's office with bars on the windows. He saw liquor stores, dry cleaners, parking lots, the State Office of Unemployment, and an auto repair garage that specialized in BMWs and Mercedes Benz.

By the time he reached Polk Street darkness was descending. Zumpo passed a steam bath that rented saunas and hot tubs by the hour to faggots. On Turk Street, he tipped his eagle feather hat to a blond-haired, black-skinned prostitute who asked him if he wanted a date. But he had learned from past experience that prostitutes only sold sex, not love, so he asked her if she had any spare change.

"Get the fuck out of here you fucking Indian queer."

He'd heard that one before, too.

At the corner of Sixth and Natoma Streets Zumpo went into Livpreet Singh's little store. Livpreet himself stood behind the counter wearing a turban and a red, San Francisco 49er jersey with the number eighteen on it. In 1947, Livpreet, with his parents and brothers and sisters left Punjab for the home of the brave and land of the free in order to escape the butchery of Partition.

When Zumpo saw Livpreet he put his hands together in an attitude of prayer and made a little half bow, which he figured was proper amongst Sikhs. "Go 'Niners," he said, by way of greeting.

Livpreet Singh put his big wide-receiver hands together just like Zumpo and made a half bow in return.

"Gene Washington is my savior," he said.

They talked football for a while, and Zumpo told him how he'd once been a football coach, even though it was not exactly true. He'd volunteered to coach the offensive line at his old school, Gardnerville High, but when some white vice principal found out he'd been expelled in tenth grade, he was told he was no longer needed. He bought a bottle of Night Train from Livpreet as they talked. When he stepped outside again he opened the wine and took a swig.

He saw a beautiful white woman receding away from him down Natoma towards the music of Howlin' Wolf. She wore boots like his, jeans like his, and a leather jacket as black as a raven. There were gold stars in her ears and four more in her right cheek, but it was her hair that melted Zumpo's heart—a green mohawk, three inches high, bold and proud.

"Wait, please miss!" He stumbled and took a nose-dive onto the stinging asphalt.

She came back and bent over him. "I'm late for rehearsal," she said. "Are you okay?"

"No," he said. "My wife ran off with a weasel. She took White Dog and my VW Westfalia camper."

"You have a Westfalia camper?"

"Not anymore," he told her.

nine

On one corner of Mac Jenks' black metal desk stood a small, framed snapshot of four green clad orderlies standing in front of the main entrance of 3rd Field Hospital, Saigon. Between the green men who stood in the center of the photo, a woman stood smiling in a wedding-gown-white nurse's uniform. A setting Asian sun shined into their eyes causing all of them to squint against it. Mac held a manila file folder in his hands, a hospital record of some sort. These five friends shared a certain longing then and, in the evening of certain bloody days, they consumed gallons of hard drink to bring about the happy swoon of goodnight. They'd all vowed to stay in touch, but the reach had been too far, too long, and Mac missed them down to his shoes.

In front of the framed snapshot lay a pile of past due bills and past due billings, paper clips, broken pencils, a small desk calendar. Mac was sick of it: the bands, the bills, the concrete walls, the stark shades of fluorescence, the gloom of faint sunlight through four dusky windows. He was sick of getting shown the door at comedy clubs: one in San Francisco, one in Oakland, another in San Jose. He was sick of winos in the alley. He was sick of Joey Wooten, the Little Surfer Boy. Worse, he was even sick of Robin, his bride, his old lady, his ball and chain. He was sick of her talk about babies and white picket fences. Mac didn't want a son. He'd seen what patriotism did to sons.

Now, he stood in front of the cracked mirror in the industrial strength bathroom, brushing his teeth. A new comedy club had opened in the Castro, and he was planning a reconnaissance in strength. Between brushes and spits, he practiced a new monologue about being an army brat. Brush, spit.

Now, he stood in front of a weary, old gymnastics mat that he'd had since he was a kid, a Christmas present from mom and dad. It lay not far from his metal desk in the wide-open spaces of the second floor. He did some stretches on it to limber up. He squatted down. He did a simple forward roll but couldn't finish standing. He went slowly. He tried several more times. Too much booze, too much sitting on his butt, too many cigarettes.

He tried some backward rolls from a squat. He wanted to recapture the gymnastic skills he'd once possessed that separated him from the usual, fat, bullshit standup comics. They were rife in these days of gas shortages, accelerating inflation and punk rock. When he got out of the army, he'd been loose and agile. Then he'd met Robin.

Later, in the rehearsal space where the concrete walls overflowed with cold, Paula Krauss of Paula and the Pistols paid Mac the wad of money she owed him.

"I'm loaded," she told him. "But, God, was I ever scared. Flying KIN to SFO with all that hash? I tell you, I was afraid I'd pee my pants."

Paula, pretty Paula. Tall and ample. Mac wondered if she'd been able to get through customs simply by flashing a come-hither smile.

"Never again," she said. "Once was enough."

Mac counted the cash.

Now, he nailed more one by fours across the yawning opening of the empty elevator shaft on the third floor. Robin was sleepwalking again so strengthening the barriers on all the landings was a necessity. A doctor at Kaiser Permanente had told her to cut down on the alcohol, cut down on the carbohydrates and get some exercise. Mac was still hammering when Robin came home.

"Those will do a fucking lot of good," she said, of the additional one by fours.

He looked askance at her with two nails still in his mouth. "I'm doing it for you, sweetheart," he mumbled.

Somnambulism, he knew, was fairly common and generally not harmful. The doctor had advised Robin to sleep on a ground floor but that wasn't possible, and he couldn't do much about the long flights of concrete steps either.

"Thanks loads, *honey*," she said, continuing up towards orange-carpeted living room, the industrial strengthen bathroom, the thin walled bedrooms.

Now, Mac stood at his homemade gun range firing his little .22LR revolver at a target pinned to the cardboard boxes filled with egg flats. On his last, tired shot he missed badly and drew concrete.

It was Friday night, late, and there being no bands rehearsing, Time & Space was filled up with a wonderful silence. Sheila McCarthy drifted in still dressed in her work clothes, slacks and jacket. She plopped down on one of the deep, old couches that faced his desk apparently exhausted.

"Male or female?" Mac asked.

"Male," she said. "The son of a bitch was nice enough at Harrington's. Bought me drinks, you know, the whole thing. Appetizers even. So I went home with the son of a bitch." Mac waited for the inevitable. "Just like all you guys."

"Hey, don't blame me. Start picking up women again." He loaded the pistol for her. "Want to take a few shots? Let off some steam?"

"Yeah sure," she said. "Where's Robin?"

Mac slipped a sixth cartridge into the cylinder and closed the loading gate. "She and Joey-boy went to the movies."

"And ice cream after, I suppose." Sheila said.

"Probably so."

Now, the two lay on Mac's gymnastics mat. A thin blanket covered them. It was too cold to lie naked on the old mat, surrounded by gray concrete, fluorescence and the reek of gunpowder. Mac asked her if she felt any better.

"I always do," she said, with an arm around his neck, trying to squeeze him closer.

The quiet was broken by the clatter of keys in the lock and the steel door opening. Joey-boy and Robin. Mac quickly tugged his pants on and slipped into his old, gray pullover sweater. Sheila grabbed her clothes and disappeared into her darkroom. They had gone through this drill any number of times before and were getting good at it. To each other they admitted, frankly, that their affair was not for love, but only for pleasure, and that the clandestine nature of it made it all the more intoxicating.

By the time Robin found him, Mac was reloading his pistol.

"Where's Sheila?" she asked.

"In her darkroom, I think."

ten

Cocaine came into fashion among young, urban whites at the same time as disco and dance clubs. Wild-haired Bobby Sun hated disco, but it just so happened that his uncle Chan had become a bona fide cocaine smuggler, and on a certain Sunday night in the great, golden City, wild-haired Bobby brought a half ounce of the stuff into Time & Space to pay Mac the money he owed, with interest.

The traditional Sunday ping-pong tournament was already raging when Bobby climbed the concrete stairs. Roily Bitches' hard rock, decibels dangerous, roared, and the cheap red wine flowed like water from the busted water heater. Bobby brought the coke in a plastic Biohazard bag that had a zip lock and was stamped all over with orange danger warnings.

He used Mac's army nickname. "Pretty funny, eh Jinx?"

Mac cracked a well-worn one liner. "Cocaine dealers, *always sticking their business in other people's noses.*"

Mac sat on one of the threadbare couches that faced a glass-topped coffee table. Red-haired Sheila

McCarthy sat beside him with her calico cat smooth on her lap. Robin and Joey Wooten had been rallying a ping-pong ball back and forth on the forest-green aluminum ping-pong table. Now, they just stood gawking at the plastic bag heavy with shinny off-white coke.

"Straight off the brick," Bobby Sun said. "Only cut once with Lidocaine. You want to chop it up, Jinx?"

Mac said he didn't want to use a razor blade. He glanced at Robin, and she understood.

She laid her ping-pong paddle on top of the ping-pong ball, went into the cockroach-infested kitchen, and fetched a small Wedgewood mortar and pestle that had once been her mother's.

Out of courtesy, Bobby Sun got the first two hits, then Sheila. Robin snorted up the two biggest lines that were left. She sucked the stuff up from so deep in her throat she sounded like a hog. The others laughed, but she felt energy again. Her heart pumped faster, her blood pressure rose to hypertensive, and she had an absolutely brilliant idea. There was a box of Flex Straws in the kitchen. A cheery pink box with Flex Straws in more colors than the rainbow peeking out through a clear plastic window. Again she trod down the narrow, sheetrock hall, past the industrial strength bathroom that smelled of urine and puke—a far cry from the friendly, springtime home she wanted, the one with chintz curtains and botanical prints on the walls.

She opened the drawer where the straws were, and someone said, "Robin." She flinched and turned. There was a strange woman sitting at the kitchen table smoking a cigarette and drinking coffee. It was not the woman she'd seen in the mirror. This one reminded Robin of Madge, a woman she'd seen in a sitcom on television, except she was fatter and older than that woman. She coughed a rattling, smoker's cough and offered Robin a seat at the table.

"Take a load off, girl. You're my favorite, you know."

The steam from the woman's coffee and the gray smoke from her cigarette mingled and rose up, and up climbing to the ceiling then rising through it into a washed out, starless city sky. Robin didn't scream. She hated horror movies in which the ingénue was so vapid she'd let out a scream at the drop of a hat or the turn of a screw. With measured calm she opened the sticking drawer where the knives, forks and spoons were kept. She lifted out the open box of Flex Straws—pink, blue, red, yellow, more colors than a rainbow sky. Returning back with Flex Straws in hand, she walked around the far side of the kitchen table.

"Same old, same old," the fat old woman said.

As she hurried back down the narrow, sheetrock hall, Robin wondered; if she was the ingénue, then who was the blue-eyed prince who would rescue her?

eleven

It was noon in the financial district and the dawn of an early spring. Tourists clad in short pants and wrap-around sunglasses stood in orderly lines at the cable car turntable on Market and California. One car had already been turned and, filled with a boatload of anatomically modern humans, began rumbling through the flatlands of the financial district. In its middle cabin, the car was equipped with facing benches and leather straps to hold onto. In the open-air sections there were outward facing benches and vertical, stainless steel handrails. Bold young people gripped those one-handed, leaned back and swung around like monkeys.

Office workers, pale from lives spent under fluorescent light, occupied the concrete ravines between tall buildings. They sat wherever they could, on benches in concrete plazas, on the concrete itself and even on various random patches of green. They ate mayonnaise heavy sandwiches, roast beef on sourdough, pastrami on rye, turkey and chicken on white and wheat, and potato chips from small bags torn from clipper racks. They drank Coca-Colas from refrigerated deli cabinets, or Coors, Guinness or Harp. Their quiet eyes watched the world glide by: cable cars, bike messengers, delivery trucks, armored cars. The watches of these white collar proletarians seemed to run faster during this pleasant time and as one o'clock rapidly approached more and more of them began to throw away the remains of their lunches and trudge back towards the air-conditioned, fluorescent lit, white noise skyscrapers of their livelihoods. Even the bourgeois—the brokers and managers in their plush sit-down restaurants—could not resist time's arrow. They paid their checks, said good day to the maitre d' and moved from the gentle dim of Japanese Sushi parlors into the sun-bright streets.

In Harrington's Bar and Grill two figures sat steadfast on stools at the far end of the bar—Joey Wooten, the one-time beach bum, and his ace boom-coon buddy, Gary Potts.

"I don't give a damn how late we are," Joey said. He was fed up with all of it—life, liberty, and the pursuit of pretty girls.

Both were junior underwriters in the plastic palm wilderness of an insurance company called West Coast Auto. They'd come to Harrington's with the intention of eating lunch—pan fried mountain trout was the special of the day—but as they waited for a table, they drank Wild Turkey at the bar, and after a couple of those or possibly four, the firm of Wooten and Potts decided eating lunch was nothing but a waste of time and energy.

"How do you suppose they fry trout if not in a pan?" Joey Wooten queried.

A thoughtful Potts replied, "Oh God, I'm really hammered."

More Wild Turkey followed and Joey's facial features began to change. His eyelids slid lower and lower, covering more and more of his eyes. His cheeks, his jowls, and mouth drooped. He began to sulk and at last fell into an alcohol induced melancholia.

"Do you know what that bitch said?"

"Yes," Potts replied. He'd been told the tale as they worked at their desks that morning, been told it again as they descended from the 18th floor in an elevator fat with other drudges then again along the same streets where the pasty proletariat sought the sun.

"You're fucked up Potts."

"You too, Wooten."

The tale of what "the bitch" said went like this— three days ago the phone on Joey Wooten's desk rang, an event that occurred many times in the course of a day. He considered the pros and cons of answering. He had just decided in the negative when he happened to look down the long ranks and files of desks before him, towards his supervisor's glass cubicle. There, Susan Rosenberg, the bitch herself, pointed repeatedly at her phone, then mimicked the act of picking up the receiver, a gesture whose meaning was obvious.

Joey answered. "Wooten, Underwriting."

She asked him if he would like to have lunch with her at Harrington's.

"My treat," she said.

A few minutes before noon, the time when he and his fellow lemmings migrated en masse, Joey hobbled with them towards the elevators. By 12:05 he was out the revolving doors and on the sidewalks weaving a path through the wriggling throng. By 12:10 he was at Harrington's. Loud talk and laughter. The long polished bar was nearly hidden by the mob of three-piece suits surrounding it. There weren't any seats left. Joey Wooten managed to balance on the tiptoes of his good right foot and crane his neck. Susan Rosenberg had left early to get a table and now she waved at him from way in back, by the kitchen.

She was maybe thirty-five years of age, an "older woman" in Joey's mind, but for him this only added another element of allure to her persona. Years before, she'd been a hippie. She'd lived on some sort of commune in the foothills of the Sierras. She'd even gone to India to look for God, but it turned out she hated the place—too many flies. Beyond that she was divorced, a wee bit on the stocky side, and her hair always seemed mussed, a phenomenon Joey did not understand. She wore little round, wire rim glasses, and Joey found her witchingly attractive.

Susan had already ordered for him, a burger and a beer. She'd already started eating and was almost done, in fact—pan-fried mountain trout. They made small talk for a minute or two—the Giants, the office, *The Sting*, with Paul Newman and Robert Redford—until Joey's burger and beer showed up. Then, Susan dropped the bomb.

"You're a great guy, Joey, but you're just kind of, well, you know." She paused, and as Joey bit into his burger, a narrow slice of tomato squirted out.

"The bottom line is that … well, I suppose you've probably figured it out by now."

Joey picked up the tomato and tried to wedge it back into his burger. "Figured what out?"

"You see, Joey … In case you don't already know, well, the bottom line is that Aaron and I are getting back together."

"Aaron? Your ex-husband?" Joey said.

"Yes, Aaron, my ex-husband. You see Joey, something I told you wasn't quite right. I sort of said I asked him to leave."

"I don't get it," Joey said.

"Well, it was him who asked *me* to leave, more or less."

"More or less? You mean he threw you out?"

Susan Rosenberg's face turned red. "I wouldn't put it exactly like that."

"Can't we talk about this?"

"We *are* talking about it."

Now, it was one thirty in Harrington's, and the firm of Wooten & Potts figured it was time to go back to work. Just one more drink, they decided. By the time they'd had that last drink or possibly two, and finally headed back to West Coast Auto it was almost two o'clock.

"Do you know what to do if you're stuck in a falling elevator?" Joey Wooten said, as they rose towards the 18th floor. Potts just shook his head.

"You start jumping up and down ..." Joey started jumping up and down, despite his lame foot. "... and hope that when it crashes into the hard concrete at the bottom of the shaft ..."

Potts started jumping up and down too, and, for a moment, the jumping seemed like the funniest thing ever. Life was good. But when they reached the 18th floor, and the elevator door opened, a vice president gazed upon them awestruck. Wooten and Potts tried to straighten up, but instead stumbled toward their desks giggling. An ominous silence enshrouded the place—typists had stopped typing, junior underwriters had stopped junior underwriting. Life was bad, and Joey, who had stopped laughing by now, decided it was her fucking fault.

She couldn't just dump a fellow like that. She was no better than any of them, and he wanted to hurt her just as much as she had hurt him. He blind staggered towards her goddamn glassed in cubicle.

"You goddamned bitch." By now Joey was shouting. "Bitch!"

He stepped into her office. She stood up but kept her desk between them. He grabbed the receiver off her telephone.

"Remember the last fucking time you called me on this?"

Now, Susan shouted back. "What the hell are you thinking? Bad things keep happening to you for a reason."

He threw the receiver at her, but the short cord stopped it.

The manager of the underwriting department, tall but average in all other ways, grabbed him from behind, and tried to get him in full nelson. Joey pulled his left arm free and circled away. One of the building's plain-clothes men, thickset as cinder blocks, grabbed at Joey's neck and easily slipped him into a headlock. After that, all the fight went out of him.

"Oh Joey, Joey," Susan Rosenberg said.

"What about Potts?" Joey managed to say.

"Don't worry about Potts. Worry about yourself. Do you want to die or something?"

"Susan ..." moaned golden-haired Joey Wooten, who had once loved beach volleyball and ocean swimming.

twelve

George Zumpo stepped into Livpreet's Corner Grocery and Livpreet put his big wide-receiver hands together and made a little half bow. "Go 'Niners," he said.

Zumpo made a little half bow in return saying, "Gene Washington is my savior." He glanced at the shelves behind Livpreet looking for Wild Irish Rose which, recently, had been fortified with ginseng to give the consumer energy. But there was none.

Livpreet apologized. "'If I knew you was comin', I'd have baked a cake.'"

Instead of Wild Irish Rose, Zumpo bought Cisco Red, which was made from anti-freeze and Robitussin. He had heard that Cisco Red made Mexicans go nutsy-crazy, but he'd never heard of it harming a *Wa-She-Shu Numu Siciliano*. Except once, when he was camped on the concrete banks of the L.A. River, he hallucinated that his dead grandmother went surfing past him on a coffin lid. "Come on in, Georgie boy, the water's fine!"

He stepped out of Livpreet's store and immediately began to fortify himself. Eddie Birdsong, the Road Chief, had discovered the address where Charlie held Leela, his dog, and his Volkswagen Westfalia camper hostage, and

Zumpo was determined to take the weasel by the horns. He slipped the Cisco Red into an inside pocket of his Salvation Army greatcoat, and Zumpo, the great walker, began his trek. All the way down Howard Street the air smelled of gasoline. The gutters were full of the stink and flotsam of the City: soda cans, beer cans, old newspapers, a dead cat, cigarette butts. He tried to keep to the "sunny side of the street" as the great Louis Armstrong advised but one side of Howard Street was just like the other and neither was particularly sunny.

Before long he passed under the ramps of a great highway and sat down to rest in the clear-cut world beneath. He sat behind a concrete pillar and drank some wine and hatched a plan. Charlie Weasel was half Mexican after all, and if Zumpo could only get him to drink enough of the magical wine, the wily weasel would turn into meatloaf on a plate.

He sat for awhile and drank for awhile thinking of the meatloaf Leela sometimes made. He remembered the nights when they'd sat at table and shared food and cheap red wine, imagining themselves to be more than they were. He drank more wine as he walked, dreamed more fanciful dreams, and by the time he got to the weasel's flat, the Cisco Red was gone.

2786 1/2 22nd Street was half underground, a suitable den for a rat like Weasel. There were iron bars on the windows and an iron gate across the front door. He descended three short stairs and stumbled. He feared all the wine would make him appear foolish and half-witted, still, he pushed the doorbell. Leela opened the door but stayed behind the locked gate.

"Georgie! How did you find me?"

"A little birdsong told me," Zumpo said.

"A what?"

It had been a stupid joke, but Zumpo never could resist telling a joke that nobody would understand. He felt dizzy from wine and his nerves were jangled. He put his hand on the stucco wall to keep his balance.

"I've come to say goodbye," he said, although he really didn't mean it.

"Goodbye?" Leela was wearing her nurse's uniform, all white, and she looked ever so pretty.

"I think I'm going away," Zumpo said. He thought for a moment. "Like Pine Ridge maybe. You know. Preach Jesus to the Oglala."

"You? Jesus?" she said. "Have you been okay, Georgie? Are you watching your salt? How's your blood pressure? You'll end up killing yourself if you keep drinking like you do."

Zumpo changed the subject. "Are you a nurse now?"

She put on the big smile he had always loved so much. "Not yet, but I'm getting closer. I'm going to be an L.V.N."

Zumpo's drunken brain dredged up a comeback. "L.V.N's are needed in Dresslerville Colony," he said. Dresslerville Colony was trailers on blocks, drunks, wild dogs, addled ex-soldier boys, old women, dirty children, and water from an irrigation ditch. Still it was better than being a Rez Indian.

"No Dresslerville for me," Leela said. "No Sagetown either. There's nothing in Dresslerville for me, except me being stuck there while you go off to heaven knows where."

"You could come with me," Zumpo said.

"Charlie's a good man, and he's got a real job."

"Doing what? Stealing chickens?"

"He's a pest control technician. Commercial pest control. You know, restaurants and things like that, so he works nights. It pays good and there's benefits. Please, Georgie, go way. Charlie's asleep. We're going to get married."

"You can't marry Charlie Weasel. You're married to me."

"No I'm not. You signed the papers when you were in prison, and quit calling him Charlie Weasel. His name is Charles Sanchez."

"I was never in prison," Zumpo said, angry now. He grabbed the iron bars on Leela's door-gate, shaking them like a gorilla in a zoo.

She took a step back. "Don't you threaten me. You were too in prison, and the marriage was annulled. You signed the papers."

"I was in jail," Zumpo said. "Jail is different from prison. And they made me sign lots of papers even though I was innocent."

Zumpo had landed in Douglas County Jail because one Saturday night in the waste of time gone by, he and his cousin Johnny Sam had gone to a basketball game at the Indian Colony in Carson City. While they were driving back to Dresslerville the tribal police—who were even worse than the white police—came after them with a vengeance. Sirens wailed. Red lights flashed. The two of them were a little drunk on Ripple, and Johnny, who owned a 1969 Chevy Malibu with a 350 cubic-inch V8, floored it.

"We'll show these *esatogus*," Johnny said, which Zumpo thought might mean police dogs in *Numu* but he wasn't sure. Nobody spoke *Numu* or *Wa-She-Shu* anymore, not even Johnny Sam. Why would they? What was the point?

They roared off screaming war whoops, "*Banzai!*" and they would have gotten away and lost those *esatogus* somewhere in the Indian Hills, if Johnny hadn't missed a turn and put the Malibu in a ditch. And then there was the stolen handgun the police claimed Johnny had thrown out the window, and that old court date Zumpo had simply forgotten about. Zumpo pled guilty on the advice of a so-called public defender that promised him he'd get probation, but the judge was a female whose fingernails were red as road kill.

"Do you have anything to say for yourself, Mr. Zumpo?"

"When I was a baby," Zumpo told her, "I was exposed to radioactive fallout from the atom bomb tests at Yucca Flats. It's natural that I sometimes forget things."

The red nailed judge brought down her mighty hammer. "Six months in Douglas County Jail, and two years' probation. Can you remember that?"

Now, Zumpo sat down on the curb in front of Leela's house and pondered how he would ever get his dog and Volkswagen camper back. He heard White Dog barking in the backyard of 2786 1/2 22nd Street and hatched a plan—throw rocks at the front of the house and shout out insults as a diversion, then hop the low back fence, pick up White Dog, lift him back over the fence, throw more rocks for good measure, and escape back to the Goodwill loading dock. But White Dog was a German Shepherd that weighed over a hundred pounds, and his throwing arm wasn't what it used to be back when he'd tried out for the expansion San Diego Padres of the National League and beaned some kid from U.S.C.

Then he saw it, parked right across the street, a gray Ford van with ORKIN EXTERMINATORS in big red letters painted across the side. If he could not have Leela, his camper or his dog, he could at least take revenge. He went searching for a rock big enough to throw through the front windshield of Charlie Weasel's Orkin truck. But there were no rocks at all on this concrete street. There was a scraggly maple tree surviving in a patch of dirt in the concrete yard of 2788 22nd Street, but even in that patch there was not a single rock, and he realized how wise he had been to abandon his crafty plan for freeing White Dog. There was not even a single rock to throw through the windshield of Charlie Weasel's van, much less the dozens he would have needed to throw at Charlie's house.

He was beginning to sober up, and it was a feeling he never welcomed. But he knew there were corner stores on almost every corner in these neighborhoods so he walked up 22nd Street and sure as hell, he found one. He bought a bottle of Pabst Blue Ribbon beer. It was a high quality beer and came in a long necked bottle that was excellent for throwing. Back at the Orkin truck, Zumpo squatted down in the gutter again, drank thoughtfully and kept the beer concealed in its paper bag—like that was going to fool anybody.

When he was done with the Pabst Blue Ribbon he stood and shouted at the weasel's house. "I want my Volkswagen Westfalia camper! Community property!" White Dog began barking again. "I want my dog! I want my camper! And I want my wife." He thought for a moment. "But not necessarily in that order."

After his anger calmed he realized he had enough money for two more beers, so instead of throwing the bottle through Charlie Weasel's windshield, he left it by the curb and walked back up to the corner store.

Soon, he was peacefully seated on his curb again, meditating on Leela and how miserable his life was: Sagetown, jail, divorce, ignorance. Three minutes later a police car pulled up alongside the Orkin truck, half blocking the street. A Chinese cop, all dressed in blue, stepped out and came towards him, one hand on his gun in its holster which, Zumpo noted, was still snapped shut.

"How're you doin', there, Chief?"

Zumpo raised his hands while the Chinese cop patted down him and his greatcoat.

"I'm doing well," Zumpo said, as the cop's hands violated him.

The cop asked him if he had any identification, and Zumpo showed him a Nevada driver's license that his cousin had sold him. It had an Indian's picture on it which was good enough for the cop, who took it back to his police car and checked for warrants. A second cop car pulled up, blocking the street all the more.

"You probably shouldn't hang around here, Chief," the Chinese cop said.

"I was just resting. Is that allowed?"

"Don't get smart with me, Chief."

The Chinese cop made Zumpo pour what was left of the third bottle of Pabst Blue Ribbon into the patch of dirt where the scrawny maple tree stood and place all the empty bottles in a proper trash receptacle back on the corner by the corner store—routine police harassment.

"Gotta keep the streets clean," the cop said.

"Indeed so. Yes," Zumpo answered. "Cleanliness is next to Godliness. The early bird catches the worm. The only good Indian is a dead Indian."

"Watch it, Chief."

"Yes sir," Zumpo said. A phony driver's license would only take an Indian so far.

It was three miles, more or less, from 22nd Street back to Sixth and Natoma, but three miles was a piece of cake for Zumpo, the great walker. He saw many interesting sights along the way that he had not noticed when he was flying high on the Cisco: laundromats and graffiti, a mural painted in the Mexican style, a Whiz Burger stand. When he turned onto South Van Ness, the same Chinese cop that had hassled him on 22nd Street slowed his cop car and watched. Zumpo waved. The cop flipped him off.

Zumpo figured it was possible that the cop had just happened by when he was sitting on the curb outside 2786 1/2 22nd Street. The cop could have happened by, seen him, and decided to harass him on general principles. He didn't think Leela would have called the cops on him, but Charlie Weasel, who wanted to be white, would have—"Some goddamn redskin is boozing it up in front of my house."

Zumpo saw a little green park at Seventeenth Street and walked through it—children, mamas, dogs, softball, but nowhere to pee. Just beyond there was some digging going on in the street, and Zumpo took advantage of the blue portable toilet there.

"Hey, asshole," one of the construction men yelled. "What the fuck do you think you're doing?" He was a black man who wanted to be white, just like Charlie Weasel. Everybody wanted to be white except for George Zumpo who only wanted to be Indian.

"Spare change?" Zumpo said.

The construction man grunted and shook his head. "Fuck you."

When he was almost back to the safety of Skid Row, Zumpo caught the scent of winos in the gentle breeze. After that he smelled dumpsters and rotting fish and heard sad voices and drunken ones. He heard some harsh ones but no police or growling dogs. In front of The Bottom of the Mark Tavern at Sixth and Howard a wino in a red Hawaiian shirt gave him a blown up paper bag with nothing inside it but air.

"Thanks man," Zumpo said. He popped it with his hands, and the wino laughed.

Just across Sixth a handful of bearded, dirty, baseball capped men squatted on the cement sidewalks in front of SOMA Mission. Zumpo thought to join them, but he had enough money left for another bottle of Cisco Red.

Pastor Jimmy Huang, opening the doors of the mission, called out to him. "George Zumpo! Come and be saved!" When Zumpo ignored him, Jimmy jumped up and down on the sidewalk like an ape, scratching his armpits. "Zumpo! Hey Zumpo!"

Zumpo yelled at him. "What the hell kind of fucking priest are you?"

"A Methodist," Pastor Jimmy called back.

Zumpo bought a bottle of Cisco Red at Livpreet's—"Gene Washington is my savior"—then walked back to his home under the Goodwill loading dock and drank Cisco Red until he began hallucinating.

His *nonna*, Mama Giulietta, shook her finger in his face. "You can't pitch, can't box, can't coach offensive line. How come you're not more like Jim Thorpe?"

thirteen

Robin had had trouble falling asleep ever since she'd come to the City of the Golden Gate. Some nights she lay in bed, while her clock radio flicked through the hours, minutes and seconds before she had to get up and go to work. Sometimes she fell asleep an hour or so before the alarm went off. Then she had to struggle to wake up, get up, drink up her tap-water instant coffee, take a broken-water-heater shower, and finally head out in her sneakers, for speed, carrying her platforms in her bottomless shoulder bag. Winos, flashers, smog. The Daily Grind.

One Tuesday night in spring, when Paula and the Pistols were blasting out hard rock, she lay in bed watching her life flash past like the numbers on her conjoined clock and radio. Now, it was midnight and they still hadn't stopped—the same goddamn song every time— "One hard climb to that crystal city ..." She just had to get to sleep before Mac came in and wanted to fuck. She slipped open the little drawer in her bedside table and fished out a bottle of Seconal, little red pills, 100 milligrams of sleep.

She froze when Mac opened the door.

"You shouldn't take that shit," he said.

"I've got to get some sleep. Can't you make 'em shut up."

"They'll be out of here pretty soon," he said, "and we need the money."

"Don't band guys ever have to work?"

"I'll go talk to them," Mac said.

When he was gone she got out her red pills again. There was a moment, perhaps thirty seconds or more, the instant before sleep came, when she felt wonderful. It was like falling into something—a dream or a deadfall, maybe. She took two of the pills, because two worked better than one, and after that wonderful instant came she began to dream that happy old, discredited dream of a kitchen that stood at the center of things, of sunlight slanting through curtained windows, of two blond-haired, wheat-haired boys playing with fire trucks on a spotless floor. The coffee cups were always full, and there were cookies and cakes. The neighbors came and went, but always laughing, and it was "Hiya, Robin," and "Whatcha doin', Madge?" Good, old reliable Madge. Good-natured. Good humored. A little cynical, sometimes, but always ready with a joke and a smile.

"Hmmmm," Madge said. "Maxwell House, 'good to the last drop.'"

They both laughed, and Madge asked if she could have some cream. Robin pushed herself up off the vinyl kitchen chair in the egg-white breakfast nook and went to the fridge.

"Would milk be okay?" Robin said. The fridge was so filthy inside she held the door so Madge wouldn't see. "There's plenty of milk, but no cream."

"Oh, milk is fine."

Mac grabbed her arm. "What the hell are you doing?"

She stood in front of an open refrigerator but it was not in the dream kitchen. She was in the kitchen of the piled high dishes and the mice and cockroaches and Sheila's day old white cake.

"What the hell are you doing?"

Robin guessed. "Sleepwalking?"

The next morning, the alarm went off like a bomb. Robin made her instant coffee. She went into the industrial strength bathroom and took her shower. The water was actually hot and she lingered for a few precious moments. She went to one of the sinks. For the first time, she was afraid to look into the big, cracked mirror. After she brushed her teeth, she finally summoned up the courage to look into the mirror. She saw nothing except herself, but she was horrified at how pale her face was, how old it looked, how haggard. She'd married too young. Even Madge, who existed only in dreams, had warned her about that.

"And no crying over spilt milk," Madge said. "You made your choice and now you're stuck with it."

"All I need is a little sun," Robin said.

fourteen

When Robin worked at the bank in San Bernardino, and Mac was still a hospital orderly in Vietnam, the City's Castro District became an oasis for gay life. The ultra-liberal inclinations of the hippie movement and its acceptance of taboo sexual practices, drew gay males, first, to the dancing-electric Haight-Ashbury. Later, when drugs turned the Haight acidic, the gays went "over the hill" to the Castro district, and the Castro was reborn, shaped into something new and vibrant.

Now, hole in the wall cafes boiled over with business. Piroshkis. Pizza. Chinese takeout. Cool cocktails, diffuse light and warm bodies filled the bars: Twin Peaks, Midnight Sun, Elephant Walk and Moby Dick. The marquee on the Castro Theater, a movie palace of the old school, read "Coming Soon: A Tribute to Bette Davis." Halfway down the block, young men pumped iron in a brightly lighted, mirrored and plate glassed muscle parlor. Next-door were the Tiberian Baths, curtained, dark and secretive.

Robin loved it. So free. So Bohemian. So San Francisco.

She sat at a table at a new comedy club called the Laff-a-Lux looking out the big picture window. She loved watching the hustle and bustle pass by: leather boys, lesbians, dykes, fairy queens, gorgeous femmes, even heteros and hippies. It was Open Mic Night and Mac was going to do a new routine in what would almost amount to an audition. He'd put on clean Levi's, a fresh shirt and had even given himself a close shave, no stubble. He looked as handsome and manly as he had when he walked into Robin's bank in "San Berdu."

"Nobody's looking," Mac said.

Robin had a pint of Old Taylor hidden in her handbag, and the waitress and the bartender had their backs turned. She slipped Mac the bottle under the table. He took it, held Sheila's glass under the table and filled it.

"Me too," Robin said.

Everyone's parents drank when she was a girl. There had been hard drinking fathers and mothers all over her neighborhood. So what did it matter, if she and Mac drank too much. Chips off the old block was what they were.

"We've been thinking you ought to see a doctor," Mac said.

"What?" Robin said, sipping her Old Taylor.

Sheila said, "Mac and I talked it over pretty thoroughly."

"You and Mac?"

"It's the sleepwalking," Mac said. "We just want to make sure you're okay."

"You want me to see a shrink?" Hot blood rushed into Robin's face.

"A psychologist," Sheila said. "Well, maybe."

"No," Robin said. "So I sleepwalk. Lots of people sleepwalk. So I went out of body once. The Maharishi can just will himself to do it. Like George Harrison. And what the hell are you doing? You two go fuck each other and then make decisions about *my* health?"

That stopped that, but before Robin could really let them have it, the cocktail waitress came over to their table—short black skirt, white blouse, tall and leggy. She asked Robin for "the bottle."

"We're not going to kick you out or anything," she said. "Just start ordering your drinks from me."

At the other end of the room, opposite the picture window was a huge "Mask of Comedy," open mouthed and laughing, that divided the playhouse from the bar. When the show started, Robin and the others walked through the Mask into the playhouse. It was like entering a dark cave. She stumbled. Mac caught her arm.

"Maybe we ought to cut you off," he said, trying to make a joke of it.

"I'm already cut off," Robin told him.

There were little, round cocktail tables, a dozen of them, black and almost invisible in the darkness. Even the little stage was black and dark—a microphone on a stand, a stool, a tangle of electrical cords, a single, focused spotlight shining down. Straight people, gays, lesbians. Two femmes sat quietly drinking and waiting, the tips of their cigarettes glowing red. One was a blonde whose skin was alabaster; the other a black woman whose skin was so dark it was almost blue. They were so beautiful and so beautifully dressed—long, high-waisted cocktail dresses. Robin had on her tightest Levi's and a peasant blouse, which looked simple and good but couldn't compare.

Mac and Sheila slipped into a curved booth in a far corner. Robin followed, but she felt herself floating away like she'd done at Harrington's at Christmas. Her hands started trembling. She tried to stop them—mind over matter, like the Maharishi, like George Harrison. But the harder she tried, the worse the trembling became, and she felt her innards churn.

"I'm going to the bathroom," she finally said.

Sheila said, "Do you want some company?"

"No!" Robin said.

The ladies' room was nothing like the industrial strength bathroom at Time & Space. It was tiled in shades of darker and lighter gray. A three foot high, sculpted mask of tragedy was done in relief on one wall but just looking at it made her woozy. There were three stalls for toilets, all spotless white, and Robin bolted into the nearest one. She latched the door and got down on her knees. She let the eruption come, all the Old Taylor, all the pretzels and everything else she'd eaten. She stayed like that, on her knees, trembling, until she regained a little self-control.

When she stepped out of the stall, the two beautiful femmes—the alabaster one and the black one whose skin looked almost blue—were fixing their faces in the mirror.

"Are you okay?" Alabaster said.

"I'm sorry," Robin said, trying hard not to cry.

"For what?" Black/blue said. She wet a paper towel and wiped the corners of Robin's mouth clean of vomit.

"Crying helps sometimes," Alabaster said.

Black/blue hugged her and held her, kissed her cheek, but Robin pushed herself away. She was a girl from Glendale, from the right side of the tracks, not some lesbian queer. She had a husband. There should have been children. There should have been a little white house with picket fences, wall-to-wall carpets, and botanical prints hanging from the walls.

"You'll be okay," Alabaster said.

When the crying stopped Robin did feel better—perfectly sober, no hallucinations, no hopes, no dreams. She stumbled out of the ladies room. She almost fell at the entrance to the playhouse—the gaping mouth of the Mask of Comedy. She braced herself against it to avoid falling and stood there, hand against the Mask while the blood pressure in her head equalized with the rest of her.

The leggy waitress went by. "Please don't touch that," she said.

"Oh, sorry."

The femmes ignored her as she passed by their table. It was, of course, impossible for them to have gotten back to their table before her and without passing her at the entrance. She sat down in the booth where Mac and Sheila were, and an instant later she wondered if she had ever left it. No more hallucinations, no more out of body—no more, no more, no more.

"Oh God. I don't think I can do this," Mac said.

Butterflies. He always had butterflies. "You'll be fine," she told him. "You always are, you know."

After the first comedian—who was too nervous to be funny—had come and gone it was Mac's turn. He didn't look back. He just went up on stage, a beer bottle in hand, and set that on the wooden stool. He adjusted the microphone for height even though it didn't appear to need it. The audience was tense and quiet—a clink of ice in a glass, a cough, a match striking.

Then, Mac pretended to trip over the cords to the microphone. He did a little skip and jump and then a Chaplin-like pratfall and fell flat on his back with a bang-slap. The crowd broke out in laughter. Mac lifted himself up but stayed half bent over, and reprimanded the audience for laughing at a man's pain, then tripped over the cords again and did a magnificent face-first fall. He rolled over, sprawled on the floor, and the audience laughed all the harder.

Robin laughed as loud as any of them and, without really wanting to, she fell in love with him all over again.

"You bastard," she thought.

He told some stories about being an "Army brat." He said how he'd been raised a flag-waving patriot who wanted to do something for his country. So he enlisted.

"Medical Corpsman, MOS 657, and I'd lucked out, or thought I had, 3rd Field Hospital. Saigon, the Paris of the East ..." He shaded his eyes and peered through the lights.

"Anybody from Saigon out there? Raise your hand, come on, don't be shy ... Saigon, what a city. Booze and bar girls. Bob Hope and Joey Heatherton flying into Tan Son Nhut ... That's what we were fighting for ... Bob Hope."

The routine was all new and hilarious—a travelogue by Monty Python. He peered through the lights again. "Anybody out there remember the Battle of Saigon? Charlie was overrunning the whole fucking city—the American embassy, the Presidential Palace. We had three guards protecting the whole fucking hospital, and two of 'em were stoned. My orderlies and me rounded up an old M-14, a Colt .45 and that was it ... Ambulances started coming in from Tan Son Nhut ... No more Joey Heatherton ..." There was still laughter, but it was nervous and scattered. When Mac started talking about the wards— festering wounds, young men without eyelids, young men who died bravely—Robin's back went stiff—amputations, "Dear John" letters, nightmares, a life no longer understood.

At last the manager of the Laff-a-Lux, tall and bearded, a hip entrepreneur, short sleeved, black shirt, red tie, stepped up onto the stage and mercifully put an end to it. He took the microphone stand away from Mac.

"Thanks so much," he said. "Let's hear it for Mac Jenks folks"

The manager started applauding politely, and the gays and lesbians, the femmes and heteros all applauded too. Robin hated the condescending bastards for humiliating him. It would have been better if they had booed and given him the hook.

They went home in Robin's mellow-yellow '65 Corvair. She'd bought it when she was a teller in San Berdu. It was old and beaten up now, but it was paid for and it was hers. Mac usually did the driving—a male's prerogative, Robin supposed—but coming back from the Laff-a-Lux, Mac passed out drunk, and Robin took the wheel.

They'd closed the Laff-a-Lux down. Two a.m., so there wasn't any traffic to speak of, a few buses, a trolley, a Yellow Cab, a drunk going way too slow. She honked, and Mac woke up in the backseat.

"Drive careful," he mumbled. He tried to crack wise but passed out halfway through the joke. "The life you save ..." he said.

Robin went straight down Market, turned right onto Sixth, then made a left across a double yellow line onto Natoma, but no cops saw her. Her favorite parking place was vacant. It was an easy one, right at the far edge of the driveway into the Goodwill parking lot. She rolled across the driveway then pulled up onto the curb without any trouble. Sheila clanked the door against a big, green dumpster when she got out.

Mac woke up. "What the fuck?"

The car was a two-door, so Robin and Sheila had to drag him out of the back. They walked him along the sidewalk, their arms supporting him at the back and waist. He started shouting about what the goddamn manager of the goddamn Laff-a-Lux had told him. "'Edit more carefully.' Asshole! Goddamned motherfucker!"

Robin shushed him. "Not so fucking loud."

"There's nobody around except fucking winos, dear heart. Why shouldn't I be loud?" He started cracking wino jokes. "What did the grape say to the wino? ... *I've got a crush on you!*"

"Learn some new jokes," Robin said.

fifteen

Joey Wooten snuck a half empty, half pint of Jack Daniels into an adult theater on O'Farrell. He drank, smoked cigarettes, and watched a comparatively well-produced film. About halfway through a rather stimulating scene of two guys on one girl, he heard a loud tick-tock, and a busload of Japanese tourists stood up as one and left the same way. A little later, he slipped the half pint back into the pocket of his gray, quilted jacket, left the theater and hobbled back down O'Farrell. He was the only person on the street, and a police cruiser slowed to look him over. He hacked up some phlegm and made a show of spitting it into the gutter. Cops were all over in this pit of depravity—he laughed out loud at that one—*depravity, Japanese tourists!*

The really sleazy, nasty, low places were further down, deeper into the guts of the Tenderloin. On Hyde Street, an appropriate name if ever there was one, he came across some poor, old bastard lying face down on the sidewalk. When Joey passed him, the old wino pushed himself halfway up, onto his elbows.

"I need an ambulance," he said.

Joey always acknowledged derelicts rather than walking right by them as if they didn't exist, and he acknowledged the shit out of this one. "Call one yourself, you useless old fuck."

Just down the block from there, a pie-faced white woman, a whore by the look of her, chased a screaming little boy up Turk Street. When she was gone, Joey pulled the Jack Daniels out of his pocket, stopped walking and medicated himself. A couple of black whores in hot pants and spike heels stood in the shadows.

"Lookin' for a date, honey?"

He looked at them. "Yeah, a blonde."

The whores turned on him. "Fuck you and your blondes, you fucking cripple."

"Niggers!" Joey shot back.

He tried not to limp as he retreated away from them. But two blocks later, his foot hurt bad. By that time, he had to pee something fierce. He thought of peeing against a wall, but he was no fucking wino. He ended up pissing in a urinal in the men's/women's room of a club called the *Faux Fille*. The blue pellets in the bowl smelled like an oil refinery, same as they did at Time & Space. One of the *Faux Fille's* girls walked up to the urinal next to him, pulled out her dick and pissed alongside him. There were no partitions between the urinals, and the Fille tried to sneak a look at his dick.

"Mind your own junk," Joey said.

"I'm sorry, honey. I just thought it looked good is all."

He zipped up. She was maybe the best one he had ever seen: slender, tall, with a young face and shoulder length blond hair that was her own. Boyish, he'd say. Her black t-shirt was cropped to expose her belly button. Calvin Klein, the t-shirt read.

At the bar he had a couple of beers or maybe three. He saw her again reflected in the long mirror behind the bar. When her eyes caught his, he looked away. Later, she danced on a little stage at the far end of the place. She did a strip but never showed her fucking dick, and by now Joey was drunk enough to want to know. He ended up seeing it and touching it in a stall in the men's/women's room. For five bucks she jerked him off.

He had another beer and stumbled off down the street. He couldn't afford all this porno shit. The goddamn government wouldn't give him unemployment because he'd been fired, not laid-off. He couldn't find a full time job because he'd been fired so he did what he could, working out of a temporary agency for just about nothing. Every few days the goddamn agency would phone him—"Mr. Wooten?"—and get him a job for a day or two, filing or typing, the dainty things that even a cretin could do.

He came from the ocean. He came from the beach, but the City was a place for cripples, so he walked the streets like a whore. He saw a one-legged man who rolled downhill in a wheelchair. He saw a young man, white and junked up, lying in an alley beside a dumpster. He saw this white boy bend at the waist, rise halfway up then fall back, rise up again, fall back again. He talked with an albino whore who looked white. She asked him if he wanted a date, he told her he was looking for a black girl just because he thought it was funny.

Flashing red lights—two police cars, black and white, were stopped in the street, in front of a liquor store that had bars on the windows. There were sirens. An ambulance came. A little clutch of gawkers stood in front of the liquor store. The two medics dashed through and around them. Joey fell in with the gawkers, watching the cops and the medics do their thing. There was another liquor store right across the street. Joey crossed over and bought another half pint of Jack Daniels.

Hobbling again, but with his good friend Jack, he stumbled into another adult theater. This one had a peep show. Mostly naked girls viewed from inside booths that had one-way mirrors. Pornography had come a long way in the last few years.

The girls stripped and kissed each other and made it with dildos. The only blonde slapped her tits onto the glass in front of him, looked through the mirror and saw him. He was sure of it.

"Are you okay, honey?"

He creamed in his pants.

Back on the street he drank his Jack and walked towards Natoma through oceans of whores and peep shows and cars and cops. The corner drug dealer was propped up against a lamppost that had a burned out light.

"Uppers, downers," the dealer said, not as a question but merely as a statement of fact. Apparently, the dealer could tell what Joey wasn't and what he was—he wasn't a narc or a cop; he was a streetwalker, just another pervert.

He bought three Black Beauty 20's, easy on the downside. He took one, washed it down with the last of the Jack and threw the clear glass bottle across the street so it hit the wall of a residence hotel and shattered. Its remains fell, tinkle, tinkle.

He headed down Turk feeling better about his life, like he could be the master of it, but he knew it was only the Black Beauties talking. When he crossed Market Street, there were a few upright citizens still on the street, the lily white ones, the ones who overran the surf spots in summer and drove out the locals, the Susan Rosenbergs of the world and their previously estranged husbands. They all stepped aside as he approached, and he laughed so damn hard he nearly fell down.

When he came to Natoma, he didn't turn left towards Time & Space, but kept on hobbling down Sixth instead. Drunk and speeding, he realized that if he followed his nose, then turned left on Brannan, and followed his nose a while longer, it was only a couple of miles to South Beach. Except it wasn't a beach anymore—a hundred years ago it probably was—but now it was just asphalt and run down warehouses, a gay bar, a leather bar, derelicts.

sixteen

The elevator was packed, a crush of white collar workhorses. A few of them tried to make room for her but, still, Robin had to shove an arm into the middle of the front rank—"Excuse me"—and fight her way onboard. As the elevator rose some suits and pantsuits managed to debark, but getting off was as tiresome as getting on.

"Excuse me."

"Excuse me."

"Hurry up please, it's time."

Twenty-second floor, Consolidated Bankers.

"Hi, Jackie," Robin said, as she dashed past the receptionist's station.

"Morning Robin. Sleep late?" coffee-and-cream-skinned Jackie said.

"Pretty much."

She snuck into Word Processing and hung her coat in a niche right across from her supervisor's glass cubicle. Her luck was good, Fat Betty was on the phone, but just when Robin thought she'd made it, Betty put her hand over the phone's black, plastic mouthpiece.

"Good morning, Robin. Got a minute?"

Shit. "I'll be right there," Robin sang out.

She got to her desk, grabbed her standard, company issued mug and hotfooted it for the coffee room.

"Robin?"

"I'm coming, I'm coming." She hated the goddamn dyke.

She made herself a cup of half coffee, half cream, and dumped in two whole packets of sugar. She took a deep draught and felt a little dizzy, then very dizzy. All at once she found herself in a bathroom eating a Hershey bar, but it wasn't the women's room at Consolidated Bankers or the one at the Laff-a-Lux Comedy Club. It was the industrial strength bathroom of the two showers, three toilets, three sinks, and two urinals on the third floor of Time & Space.

She was in front of the big, cracked mirror that spanned the sinks, looking at two images of herself, slightly offset. The same woman she had seen months before appeared in the big, flawed mirror.

"Same old, same old," the woman said.

Now, in the flawed glass she saw herself playing ping-pong—doubles with Joey Wooten, against Mac and red-haired Sheila McCarthy.

"Two serving zero," Robin said. In real life they never played doubles, but that's what they were doing now.

"Same old, same old."

Robin woke up with her head between her knees. "Just relax, honey. Relax and breathe." Betty put a gnarled meathook of a hand on Robin's shoulder and held her down.

She was in the coffee room at Consolidated Bankers, and she was almost sure this was real, neither dream nor reflection nor fabrication.

"You go home and get some rest," Betty told her. "You got to stop burning the candle at both ends."

"I know," Robin said.

That night she took a red pill and tucked herself into bed all alone. She could hear Mac fucking Sheila in Sheila's room next door. She wondered if she ought to go fuck Joey Wooten in Joey's room. She thought of Mac's little pistol in the unlocked top drawer of his desk and wondered if she was going insane. She wondered if maybe she was insane already and everything was really a hallucination in a padded cell in Napa State Hospital. She pondered all that—cheating husbands, loveless life, and the nothingness of death—until the red pill took hold of her, and in that one, empty instant before sleep, as she tumbled into a dream, she flew—a gull in a lavender sky.

seventeen

It was a warm Sunday morning that promised to grow hot—unusual in this seaboard city—but Sheila McCarthy had talked Mac into it. He hated the complexity of heat and crowds and buildings. The cool, dark emptiness of Time & Space suited him better, but sometimes he worried over that, just as he worried over babies and razors and shaving.

"Its not really a parade," Sheila argued. "It's more like a moving party. You like parties, don't you?"

"They're okay," Mac said.

He'd asked Robin if she wanted to go, but she said she had other plans. She'd found a half busted chaise lounge at Goodwill, and she wanted to get some sun on the roof, encumbered only by a greenish plastic bottle of Sea & Ski, a book by Edgar Cayce, and a twenty-four ounce can of Colt 45.

"You guys go," Robin said. "It doesn't matter anymore."

"If that's what you want," Mac said. "But why can't the three of us go?"

"I want to be two, not three."

So Mac and Sheila walked down Howard Street, just the two of them, towards the assembly point for the Gay Freedom Day Parade. The cross streets were blocked off by police cars and motorcycles

"Cops always love to pull down overtime," he said.

"Its sad she won't go for it," Sheila said. "I mean if three people love each other, why not?"

"Too old fashioned, I guess."

"Why don't we just seduce her? Get her a little stoned, you know. She likes sex doesn't she?"

"Yes, but it's been a while."

"Does she masturbate?'

"I only talked with her about it once," Mac said. "She claims she never has and never will. She was quite adamant about it, so I didn't ask anymore."

"Weird chick."

The nearer they came to the Embarcadero, the more people filled the street—gay men, lesbian women, a half dozen shirtless bodybuilders wearing skin tight short shorts. Others came in on streetcars that humped up the Transbay Terminal ramp. The crowd filled Howard Street and flowed as steady as the Styx. It carried Mac along against his will, like wreckage on the swell. The flow took him into the dark shadows under the Terminal and the huge overpasses that spanned Howard, Folsom, and Harrison streets. The pigeons there had grown fat on the debris of sidewalks—spilled popcorn, candy corn, Cracker Jack. But as the mob grew thicker the pigeons fluttered to the safety of the high perches on the steel beams and concrete abutments. All of it, the crowd, the traffic sounds, the random flights of pigeons, the poison gas that trailed the buses, jangled Mac so bad he stopped and told Sheila he needed to rest.

"It'd be warmer out in the sun," she said.

The enormous shadow cast by the Terminal was cold as a tomb, but Mac had already slipped into a dark, concrete cranny.

"This is fine. I like it here."

When Mac had steadied his nerves, they began to walk again. A few blocks more, and they came up against the body of the beast—a chattering mob that extended from the Ferry Building all the way down Steuart past Howard and Folsom. There was a forest of homemade signs: Human Rights Are Absolute, Support Gay Teachers, End Police Harassment. Banners spanned the street: Ministers for Gay Rights, Women's Committee for Gay Rights, Santa Cruz Lesbian Delegation. Pickup trucks and cars were decked with flowers. Harvey Milk sat on top of a white Volvo, dangling his legs down through its sunroof.

Sheila had brought her almost new Pentax with a 55mm lens and plunged into the crush looking for images. Mac hung back.

"Come on, they don't bite," Sheila said.

He stayed on the sidewalk, which was crowded but not packed, and he was able to make way to the forefront of the march. A dozen motorcycle cops in four files headed it up—white helmets, mirrored sunglasses. When the clock on the Ferry Building ticked to 10:30, a whistle blew, motorcycles roared and the cops started slowly up Market. Behind them, twenty dykes riding polished chrome bikes revved their engines. Behind these were gay men and women on motorcycles and bikes, everything from deep-throated Harleys to soprano Hondas.

Mac saw Sheila in the midst of them with her fingers in her ears but grinning—drum corps and electric bands on flatbed trucks.

"Look!" she shouted. "Roily Bitches!" And there they were: Mohawk haircuts, pierced noses, cheeks and lips. Sheila waved at Mac then pushed her way through a squad of dykes escorting the Bitches. She took pictures of them, and when the Bitches finished their song—"You slit your wrist you silly bitch!"—Sheila reached up and shook the hand of the bass player, her latest infatuation.

Mac walked the sidewalk, hiding in arbitrary shadows. The head of the procession—laughing, strolling, cheering—was coming up on an Army recruiting office meaning, more seriously, that Mac was too.

He'd stoppered up his rage years ago and now, if not for the parade, he might have crossed over Market Street. He would have avoided the sergeant major who stood at the door of the recruiting office snapping pictures with a Kodak Brownie.

Mac Jenks: first tour, Ward Orderly, 3rd Field Hospital, Saigon, second and third tours, Ward Master, same place, same MOS—120 degrees Fahrenheit, the stinking burn unit, bed pans, amoebic dysentery, barbecued boys. Bob Hope. Joey Heatherton.

"How do you like the parade, sarge?" Mac tried smiling. "Not much like the parades you're used to, I'd wager."

"Not much," the sergeant said.

The sergeant: a pitchman whose belly hung out over his belt. Mac Jenks: stubble bearded and brain-fucked.

He offered the sergeant a cigarette, and the son of a bitch took it. Brain-fuck wounds came from being out of toilet paper, from being out of comic books, matches, salt tablets, dental floss, Kool-Aid. Brain-fuck wounds came from killing dogs, pigs, goats and cattle. Brain-fuck wounds came from throwing dead dogs down wells. Nothing helped brain-fuck, not Pentazocine or Demerol or morphine.

The sergeant snapped a picture of four men dressed like women from the Victorian era—parasols, broad hats, high collars, slim white dresses, elegance and grace, except that they were men and walked like it.

Sheila came up beside Mac, all smiles.

"Mind if I take your picture?" she asked the sergeant.

The sergeant gave her a lecherous smile and posed.

"No," she told him. "With the camera, taking a picture."

"I get it," the sergeant said. He posed again but with his camera aimed straight at Sheila—a picture of the sergeant taking a picture of Sheila. The two of them laughed, but Mac didn't. Cheap red wine, cocaine, nothing helped Mac's brain-fuck.

He pulled back from the edge. "You're out of shape, sarge. Trying to hide your belt buckle?"

Barbecued boys, boys who couldn't shit, boys who couldn't stop shitting.

Mac offered the sergeant his hand. "3rd Field Hospital," he said.

"Easy street,'" the sergeant said.

Mac snapped. "Why are you standing on my sidewalk, recruit?"

"Say what?"

Mac shouted. 'Why the fuck are you standing on my fucking sidewalk, recruit?'"

Sheila grabbed Mac's arm and pulled him away. She dragged him across New Montgomery and pushed him up against the wall of the Palace Hotel.

"What's the matter with you? For Chrissakes." She pulled on him again, but this time he didn't resist.

"I'm fine," he said. "I'm fine." He stoppered himself up again.

The Gay Freedom Day Parade ended just off Castro Street at Duboce Park in the Lower Haight. Duboce wasn't a large park but there seemed to be ten thousand people lounging on the grass. Mac and Sheila found some shade under a bushy tree, a space they shared with three pretty lesbians who wore heavy mascara and ate figs. Two topless young men had a Dalmatian that sprawled on the grass and rolled and rolled, scratching its itch.

Mac held out his hand to the dog. It started licking his hand then his face until it bowled him over, licking his face, nose, mouth, anything he could get his tongue on.

One of the young men tried to call the dog off. "Stop it, Jax!"

Mac said he didn't mind but got a hold on the dog's collar just in case. Sheila lay on her back in the grass with her knees bent. She raised one hand to shelter her face from the rays of the silver sun bleeding through the branches of the tree. She asked Mac if he wanted to catch a shuttle bus to the Freedom Day celebration in Golden Gate Park.

"Its too hot," he said. "Too crowded."

eighteen

July 4, 1976, the Bicentennial.

There were parades in Golden Gate Park: marching bands, equestrian units, concerts, bag pipers in kilts, visiting sailors from Australia and Korea, a march by left-wingers protesting against the rich. Fireworks were scheduled to be launched from both Candlestick Park and Alcatraz Island. Twin Peaks was clearly the best vantage point, offering spectacular views of the City, but there were risks: snarled traffic, lack of parking, fog, wind and cold.

Robin, Mac, Joey and Sheila, emboldened by Thermos bottles filled with Irish coffee, parked as near as they could, and started walking. They found a hillside trail up through the brush and coastal scrub. It had steps made from wood blocks set into the earth. It was like climbing Everest, but they had come prepared: backpacks, heavy jackets, watch caps, flashlights, even blankets.

Joey struggled on the uneven ground and the endless steps. He had to drag his left foot along, despite his brace. Mac and Sheila, the strongest and healthiest, the fit who survive, went ahead, but Joey had to rest. He sat down on the thick wood steps, and took off his orthotic shoe and adjusted his brace. Robin sat down beside him.

"To heck with 'em," she said. "We can see fine from here." She took a Thermos out of her pack and filled the cup with steaming Irish coffee and gave it to Joey.

"No cream on top," she said. "But enough whiskey, sugar and caffeine to kill demons." When he handed the cup back to her, she sampled it herself. "A little analgesic never hurt anybody," she said.

"I'm not so sure of that," Joey told her.

A group of five older people in shorts, t-shirts, and light jackets—tourists who hadn't realized how cold a hill in the City could be on a foggy night in July—came tramping down the stair step path. Robin moved closer to Joey to make room for them to pass. As they went by, a stoop shouldered man with a camera slung around his neck, stopped and asked Joey if he was okay.

"Yeah," Joey said, as he adjusted his brace. "I just need to rest a minute. Thanks for asking."

"You might save yourselves the trouble," the tourist said, inclining his head towards the steepening trail. "I don't think it'll be much of a show with all the fog." He stopped just below them on the trail and, for some reason Robin couldn't fathom, snapped their picture.

Robin took a camping blanket from her backpack, and put it around Joey's shoulders and then her own. She moved closer to him, and they huddled together against the wind until they felt warm and safe

"Cozy," Robin said. "Two peas in a pod."

They sat like that for a long time, snug and anesthetized. The sun set behind them and, in the gathering darkness, latecomers, with more heart than the tourists who'd retreated down the trail, rushed on up the steps. Whenever they passed, Robin edged closer to Joey.

"Let's just stay like this," she said.

nineteen

It was 2 a.m., "last call" at the numberless watering holes of the City. On Union Street, the upscale fern bars and dance clubs were beginning to close—glasses collected, tables wiped down, chairs set on tables, floors swept and mopped. Their sophisticated clientele, the white collar proles who worked in the tall buildings downtown, began to wobble home—some with those they'd come with, some with those they'd picked up and others, still, with no one at all.

In a sports bar called The Corner, at the intersection of Union and Laguna, the doors were locked, and the bar was closed, but a game of high stakes straight pool had begun, just like in the movies.

"How do you feel, Fast Eddie?"

"Fast and loose."

"In the gut, I mean."

"Tight, but good."

The scene on Castro Street was almost indistinguishable from that on Union. The gay bars—Twin Peaks, Midnight Sun, Moby Dick, Elephant Walk—were just beginning to empty. Slender young men in leather chaps, short shorts or even tailored suits began to wobble home, some with those they'd come with, others with those they'd just picked up. But the ones who walked singly here, still had one last gambit to play. They lined up along Eighteenth Street or sat alone in the passenger seat of parked cars, right hand window rolled down.

"Want to have a night?"

Below Market Street, in the impoverished heart of the great City, the Pastime, the Dew-Drop-Inn, and the Sports-Para-Dice were closing up too. On Sixth Street, several blocks deeper down than Natoma, there was a bar called The Ruins, where violence was common and the pool games weren't always friendly.

A man with a fucked up foot said, "You scratched on the eight ball. You didn't call the pocket."

The big man with a pool cue in his hands answered, "Bullshit. You don't got to call the pocket. You owe me a sawbuck."

"Like hell I do."

"Like hell you don't."

#

Later, George Zumpo, at rest under the Goodwill loading dock, pondered how much lower he could go, living as he did, like a reptile. Leela, White Dog, and his Volkswagen Westfalia camper all seemed lost to him now. He supposed he could go back to Gardnerville, slink in like a shamed dog, tail between his legs, laughed at by friends, haunted by grandma.

He heard the Natoma Troll issue a challenge.

"I'll knock your fucking block off. Right off your fucking shoulders. What-d'-ya think of that? What-d'-ya think?"

Zumpo stuck his head out from under the loading dock and saw the Troll shadow boxing in the small circle of light beneath a streetlamp. His fundamentals were awful.

"Tuck your chin in," Zumpo called. "Hide it behind your shoulder." Zumpo had fought eight times professionally in Reno, or maybe only twice.

The Troll reissued his challenge. "Chin down, elbows tucked. What-d'-ya think of that? What-d'-ya think?"

A drunken white man staggered out of the streetlights on Sixth, into the dark of the Natoma. The man had long yellow hair and walked with a limp. Zumpo slithered out from under the loading dock. It was the same, lame man who had given him directions once, the same lame man who lived in the building where bands played the music of Howlin' Wolf, Bo Diddly and Chuck Berry.

The white man was naked to the waist and held his shirt pressed against the left side of his face. It was wet with blood and, as the white man came towards Zumpo, he stumbled and nearly fell. He stopped not a yard from Zumpo, pulled the shirt away from his face, and Zumpo saw that a great red gash extended from his left temple almost down to his mouth.

"Pool cue," the white man told him.

"Nasty," Zumpo said.

The white man said many more words but they came out slurred and incomplete. "Eight ball … Ruins …"

The white man began to crumble. His crippled foot bent at the ankle. One of his knees gave way. As he fell, Zumpo grabbed at him, but the white man slipped through his hands and ended up on all fours. He puked out beer and pretzels, then collapsed face down and unconscious, half in the puke, half out.

When Zumpo and his blood brother Johnny Sam were volunteering to be volunteer firemen at the Topaz Lake V.F.D. the two of them had seen most of a training film about carrying people out of burning houses so

Zumpo knew exactly what to do. He got the white man flat on his stomach, squatted down up by his head, put his hands under his armpits and pulled him up. After he got him more or less vertical, Zumpo raised him up on his shoulders, and carried him proudly down the alley towards Time & Space.

"What-d'-ya think? What-d'-ya think of that, motherfuckers?" the Troll called out.

Moments later, with the white man still on his shoulders, Zumpo leaned on the doorbell. When no one answered, he laid his burden down, fished through the white man's pockets for a key then dragged him into the three a.m. concrete dark of Time & Space.

The white man puked again. Zumpo called for help. The lights went on, and a white man wearing sweat pants came down the concrete stairs. His left arm swung free, but he kept his right hand pressed against his thigh, barely concealing a cocked pistol. Zumpo figured he might be a cop, and, from force of habit, threw up his arms in surrender.

"I didn't do it," he called out. "Don't shoot! I'm innocent."

The man looked him over, put the pistol on half cock, squatted down and looked at the gash on his friend's face.

"Jesus, what the hell happened?"

"He got beat up," Zumpo said.

"I'll say he did."

The white woman Zumpo had seen pushing shopping carts filled with laundry toward the Coin-Op came down the concrete stairs wrapped in a terry cloth bathrobe. "My God! What happened?"

The man with the gun told her to get dressed. "Fast," he added. "And get your car keys. He's probably concussed."

twenty

Madge said Sheila was a slut.

"But, hell, men are men, you know. They fuck like bunnies, most of 'em, wherever and whenever. Just go into any bar on Castro Street if you don't believe me. So you've got to forgive him, forgive and forget, that's what I always say. Well, sometimes say. He's a good man, but, hell, Vietnam and all. As far as Sheila is concerned, I wouldn't give you half a fuck for her."

"She is a bit of a whore," Robin said. "With all her one night stands ... She doesn't *look* slutty, though."

"I think she does," Madge said.

They sat at a simple plank table in the middle of Madge's beautiful kitchen, drinking Maxwell House Coffee, smoking cigarettes and nibbling day old white cake. Robin loved Madge's kitchen, simple but still elegant. The counter was L-shaped, with marble countertops that had a flat blue finish. Just above the counters was a foot wide band of white tile, and above that, the walls were painted sky blue.

"The pill is liberating," Madge said. She coughed a cancerous cough. "But women like Sheila take advantage."

"Well, yes," Robin said. "But this is a new age and all. Lots of people have open marriages."

Madge leveled a finger at her. "But if it's open for him it ought to be open for you too."

Madge had smoked unfiltered cigarettes for too many years, and Robin supposed she would die young because of that, or have a heart attack as fat as she was. Still, Robin loved having her next door. She lit up another cigarette. Robin's were filtered, of course—Virginia Slims, "You've Come a Long Way, Baby." Her cough wasn't near as bad as Madge's, much less Joey's.

"That boy better shape up," Madge said. "Its hard getting fired and being out of work, but life goes on. Right?"

"He's a sweetheart, basically," Robin said. "Although he hasn't been quite right since, you know ... his accident. But wouldn't you just love to run your hands through that curly blond hair?"

"No, and you shouldn't either. If you're going to have an affair with somebody, and I don't say you shouldn't. But please, for God's sake, don't have it with someone you're already living with."

"I suppose, not," Robin said.

"And you've got to stop worrying about these experiences you've been having. They're not unnatural, they're signs of a higher mind. Develop your powers, don't fear them."

Madge's husband, Thorny, came in wearing a sport jacket and a tie, he was always so dapper and so clean.

"Hi, Robin," he said, with a big happy smile. He gave Madge a peck on the cheek. Madge turned towards him and the two played kissy-face for a moment.

"Watch out!" Robin said. "I just might try to steal him away from you someday."

They all laughed, and Thorny put a beautifully manicured hand on Robin's shoulder.

"What crazy stunts are you two girls cooking up today?"

Suddenly, the lights went on. Madge and Thorny went as pale as ghosts, turned into cigarette smoke, rose through the plank ceiling and became the night sky.

Mac's strong right hand was on Robin's shoulder, otherwise she might have flown up into the sky, too. "What are you doing?" Mac said.

Robin guessed. "Coffee and cake?" But when she looked down at the old, industrial strength tin-topped table, she saw that she wasn't drinking coffee at all, but drinking Colt 45 instead.

She tried to push Mac's hand off her shoulder. "That hurts."

"Sorry," he said, pulling the hand away. "Let's get back to bed."

Her legs were wobbly when she stood, too much out of body, she supposed. Mac slid his arm up under her armpit and supported her down the long hall to their bedroom. He put her to bed and even covered her as one would cover a child. As she lay there half asleep, falling, falling, falling, Mac told her he was going to throw her red pills away.

"Thank you," she said, wondering why he was being so nice to her.

twenty-one

It was Sunday night, and George Zumpo sat on a threadbare sofa in the orange-carpeted living room guzzling cheap, red wine. He'd been treated like a hero ever since he'd carried the unconscious Joey Wooten down Natoma and laid him on their three a.m. bare concrete floor. They'd given him lodging and fed him, much as one would a pet gerbil. They'd given him his own toothbrush. They'd bought him pre-owned jeans at Goodwill and even a fine, good as new Giants sweatshirt, which was orange with black lettering and caused him to virtually disappear when he lay inside his greasy orange sleeping bag on the thin orange carpet. He slept under the spotless, aluminum ping-pong table. He showered everyday, even though the water sometimes turned unbearably cold without warning. He had even gotten quite comfortable perusing Vogue magazine when he sat on the toilet.

"You're disgusting," Sheila McCarthy said, when she caught him at it.

Occasionally he took his meals at SOMA Mission, and was even pleased when Pastor Jimmy Huang had used him as a prop in one of his harangues—"Whoever despises his neighbor is a sinner, but blessed ..." And so forth and so on, and so forth some more.

Now, Sheila, Robin and Mac sat on the sofa across from him drinking cheap red wine while they debated the recently discovered "face on Mars."

Mac, the skeptic, took the negative side of the argument. "There's no fucking face on Mars. It's just like, I don't know, a trick of shadows and light."

Robin, the fantasist, declared that some ancient Martian race could have chiseled it out of the rock. "Like the Egyptians, you know?"

Zumpo, the fabulist, said, "My *nonna* got abducted by Martians once ... Anybody got an extra smoke?"

Sheila gave him a cigarette. She asked him what a *nonna* was.

"Its *Siciliano*. You know?" Zumpo said. "My *nonna*, my grandmother on my father's side, Mama Guilietta. She got the urge to play the slots, so she was driving down to Vegas in this cherry, '59 Chrysler Imperial—top down, wrap around sunglasses, headscarf, rosary in her lap— when ... BANG-CRACK ... the Imperial throws a rod."

"I don't believe it already," Mac said.

The ping-pong games raged that night, and Roily Bitches roared. "... I'm too fucked up to fall in love ..." But when Bobby Sun showed up with fifty pairs of earplugs, and three eight balls of cocaine, "straight off the fuckin' brick," the ping-pong was no longer relevant. They stuck earplugs in their ears—"Hey! These things almost work!"

Mac began crushing up the cocaine in Robin's mother's mortar and pestle, and told Robin to go get the Flex Straws.

"Me?" she said. "I always get 'em. Make Sheila go."

"I don't know where they are," Sheila said.

"They're in the fucking drawer," Robin told her.

Zumpo, the great walker, took the bull by the horns and made the long walk down the narrow sheetrock hall himself. He got the Flex Straws and, while he was rummaging the shelves, he found two packages of Mother's Cookies that were relatively free of cockroaches—Oatmeal Raisin and Coconut Chocolate Chip. Clutching those and the Flex Straws against his chest, he made for the orange-carpet room where Robin and Sheila were still bickering.

"I get it," Sheila said. "You only go into the kitchen when you're sleepwalking."

"Go fuck yourself," Robin told her.

Once he'd tooted a couple of lines, Zumpo had a clearness of mind he hadn't felt since the first time he ditched kindergarten. If he couldn't have Leela or his Volkswagen Westfalia camper, he thought, was it not justice for him to steal White Dog back?

"White Dog and I were best friends," Zumpo said. "We went everywhere together, the Mountains of the Moon, Death Valley, Disneyland ..."

Bobby Sun laughed. "They don't let no fucking dogs in Disneyland."

"I have powerful friends," Zumpo told him.

"I don't believe that either," Mac said.

"... the Pine Ridge Reservation, Miami Beach, Kissimmee. But those carefree days are gone forever now, because Charlie Weasel is fattening him up for the kill."

"You mean Charlie Weasel is going to eat him?" Robin said.

"That's almost like ... like ..." scar-faced Joey Wooten ran out of words. Sheila finished the sentence for him. "... Cannibalism," she said.

"The only kind of dog you should eat is a hot dog," Mac said. As usual, nobody laughed.

Bobby Sun told them he'd eaten dog once. "It wasn't bad, you know? For dog, I mean."

Zumpo said he'd eaten dog himself, in stews mostly, and had found it rich and flavorful, not like cat, which was boney and sour.

"My god," Sheila said. "How could you eat a cat? A dog I can understand, but not a cat."

Zumpo bummed another cigarette. "I was drunk," he said, that being his patented excuse for everything.

He stepped into some imaginary limelight in the middle of the room and said, "Who will go with me to snatch White Dog from the jaws of the Weasel?"

"Let's do some more coke first," Robin said.

After the rest of the cocaine was tooted, the cookies were eaten and still more wine imbibed, Zumpo and his sky-high dog raiders grabbed a half gallon of Gallo Hearty Burgundy and wedged themselves into Robin Jenks' mellow-yellow, two door, 1965 Corvair. Mac, as usual, took the wheel.

"Where the hell is this place?" he asked.

"22nd Street," Zumpo told him, pointing forward. Mac floored it. The underpowered Corvair slowly built momentum until at last they sped out of the land of winos, dumpsters and rotting fish, past the graffiti and the Whiz Burger stands, and into the world of stylized Mexican murals and taquerias. Sheila, who had been political in the Sixties, rolled down the passenger side window and called out to pedestrians, Hispanics and Anglos alike—"Free White Dog! Power to the People!"

Robin sat motionless, pinned in the rear seat between Zumpo and Joey Wooten. "Zump'?" she said. "How do you expect to fit a hundred pound German Shepherd in here?"

"Don't worry," Zumpo said, but he realized Robin's question was the first sign the cocaine was wearing off.

When they reached 2786 1/2 22nd Street, there was no place to park. Mac orbited various blocks as quickly as the Corvair's controversial rear suspension would allow.

"Slow down," Sheila said. "I'm starting to feel sick."

"Don't barf in the car," Robin said, and the bickering started again.

"I won't barf in your goddamn car."

"If you do you'll clean it up yourself."

"Fuck you."

"Fuck you back."

"You should drink some more wine," Zumpo said, passing the long-necked half-gallon over Sheila's shoulder. "It settles the stomach," he told her.

At last, Mac gave up trying to find a parking place, and settled the Corvair up against a red, curved corner, where 22nd met Florida.

Joey Wooten said, "We can't park here. It's illegal."

"So's stealing some fucking dog," Bobby Sun told him.

"It isn't stealing," Zumpo said.

"Its 'liberating'," Sheila, the ex-radical, declared.

A police car pulled up alongside them just as she thrust her head out the open side window. Zumpo nodded forward, rested his chin on his chest, hunched over, and tried to disappear. It was the same goddamn Chink cop who'd stopped him twice before.

The cop turned his spotlight on and pointed it at Sheila. "Are your okay, darlin'?" the cop said.

"Never felt better," Sheila said, and at that very moment she began to spew her guts onto the asphalt: red wine, green bile, chocolate chip cookies.

The cop turned his spotlight on Bobby Sun, the hard rocker, who knew eighteen phrases in Chinese. "*Ni Hao*, man," Bobby said.

When the spotlight fell on Mac, he leaned forward so the cop could see him better. "She's just had way too much to drink," Mac said. "Her cat died, you see, and she was tying one on in some Mexican bar out here. We went to pick her up. I just stopped in the red 'cause she was feeling sick."

"Yeah, right," the cop said. "And none of you been drinking anything?"

"Maybe a beer or two," Mac said.

The cop swung the spotlight towards the back seat and illuminated the rest of the erstwhile dog raiders, one by one.

"Good evening, officer," Joey Wooten said.

"Hello, sir," Robin said.

The light fell on Zumpo. "Chief!" the cop exclaimed. "Good to see you again."

twenty-two

Joey Wooten reckoned that the waiting room of the Berkeley Institute for Paranormal Research was nice enough. It was located in a clean, modest, one and a half story bungalow in West Berkeley. The waiting room had once been the bungalow's clean and modest living room, but, now, an imitation Persian carpet covered most of the worn down, wall-to-wall carpet. Navy blue, structured beanbag chairs provided seating. There were two little black tables topped with back issues of *New Age* and *Spirit Consciousness*. Six potted plants—Joey didn't know what kind—hung suspended from the ceiling in macramé plant hangers.

Joey sat half-slumped in one of the beanbags, hiding his pool-cue scarred face behind an incongruous issue of *Sports Illustrated*. Across from him, sat an aging hippie: sandals, worn out jeans, and a t-shirt emblazoned with "Pot is Fun" across the chest.

At last, an older man came down a carpeted stairway that led to the upper half floor—black Nehru jacket, graying hair. A retired school teacher, Joey figured.

"Madeline will see you now," Nehru said. The hippie struggled to get out of his beanbag.

Joey was there at Robin's request to give her some moral support, seeing as how Mac—the selfish bastard—wouldn't do it. Joey didn't buy any of this new age crap: the astral plane, channeling, Madame Blavatsky, Wicca, spirits. Nor had he ever thought, "Everything happens for a reason." Things happened randomly, like the accident that smashed his foot. But if Robin wanted to try psychic whatever, it was all right with him. Joey didn't know for sure, but he supposed she was suffering the natural melancholia of every defeated city dweller—every underpaid drudge filling a position on a hierarchical organization chart.

Just as he reached that conclusion, self-destructive as he supposed it was, Robin came dancing down the stairs. She dashed up to him, absolutely brimming over, as if she were spotless and new. She threw her bare white arms around his neck and pecked him on the cheek.

"She knew all about me!" Robin said. "She knew I was from L.A. She knew all about my troubles with Mac, and even that I've been having psychic experiences."

"Sleepwalking?" Joey said.

"No, no, it's much more than that. I'll tell you about it later. She even knew you were a skeptic."

"Me?" Joey said.

"She saw you when we came in. She thought you were Mac, at first, but then the skeptical friend part came through. She wants to meet you."

"Meet me? Why?"

"She'll come downstairs in a minute or two. She's just amazing."

He saw her, but she did not come down the stairs. Instead, she breezed in from the back of the house—the kitchen maybe. She was auburn-haired, in her forties, not very tall. The way she moved seemed calculated to Joey, like a poser on the beach, all show but no go. But at least there was no gypsy fortune-teller garb, no sorcerer's robes, nothing like that. She was just a regular looking, middle-aged woman, extending her right hand towards him.

"Madeline Dove," she said. It sounded like a fake name to Joey. Still, he shook hands with her.

"You must be Joey," she said.

"Joey, yes."

"How are you?" She put her left hand over their joined right hands, and squeezed. "I can tell you two are close. You both have old souls. I can weigh souls you see, just as sure as if I hung them on balance scales."

"Really," Joey said.

"You had some problems growing up, didn't you?"

Well, who didn't, Joey thought. She finally let go of his hand.

"Trouble with your father. Is that right?"

"Yeah," Joey said, contorting his mouth into something resembling a smile.

"He treated you like a child even when you were a young man, a grown up?"

"Yeah."

"And you had some illness, maybe even polio?"

"No," he said. "Not me."

"A friend of yours. Maybe even your best friend?"

"Yes," Joey said. "My best friend."

When they left, Robin said she was too excited to drive and asked Joey to take the wheel. The car had an automatic transmission, which was okay with Joey, but it also had a goofy little shifting lever coming out of the dash. He hadn't driven in some time, and he didn't find threading Berkeley's narrow streets easy, especially while still trying to converse with Robin.

"Madeline wants you to sit in when I have my next appointment," she said. "All that stuff about your father was absolutely right, wasn't it? Isn't she amazing?"

Joey didn't want to spoil things for her. "Yeah, my father was a bit rough with me, and she's right that I'm a skeptic."

"And how could she have known about your friend having polio?"

"I don't know," Joey said. It was true that as a kid he'd been friends with a boy who had polio, and it didn't seem like something a faker would be able to guess.

"Sure," he said. "I'll get a reading with you next time, if that's what you want."

Now, he wheeled the Corvair into the parking lot of a California style hofbrau down near the freeway. Inside, Joey pushed his tray down the line at the steam table with Robin close behind. He ordered his usual dish, hot roast turkey with mashed potatoes, gravy and stuffing. Thankfully, the joint had a bar. After they sat down— Robin with pastrami on dark rye, Joey with his turkey platter—he called to the barmaid and ordered a carafe of the house red.

"I'm going to quit drinking," Robin said, as Joey poured her a glass.

He stopped pouring. "Really? Why?" He pulled the bottle back. "Don't you want any?"

"Well of course I'm not going to quit this minute. I might get the DTs or something. But I am going to start tapering down. Madeline said you can't drink alcohol or take drugs if you want to develop your psychic powers, and you should do the same, Joey."

"I get a little drunk every once in a while, but I can handle it."

"Like getting fired and beat up? Just look at your face in a mirror. Your face is still a mess."

"You drink a lot, too," Joey said. "Hell, everybody does."

"I was afraid I was going crazy, but Madeline says visions and out of body experiences mean I probably have

115

strong psychic powers. But please don't tell Mac. I've got to have someone I can trust."

"Me?" Joey said. "You trust *me*?" He poured himself another glass of wine.

"Look." Robin dug a handful of rocks out of her purse and showed them to him. "We do psychic meditation with crystals."

Joey said, "Sugar is a crystal, you know."

When they were done with the wine Joey felt better, even relaxed. When they left the hofbrau Joey was a little drunk, and the mellow-yellow Corvair seemed a little easier to handle. At the merge onto the freeway, Joey floored the accelerator, which didn't have much effect. Still, he dodged right into the narrow space between an eighteen-wheeler and a fire engine red Mustang. Further ahead, car upon car merged from the left lanes into the right.

"That guy didn't even look!" Joey said. The whole thing began to remind him of the bumper car ride at the Boardwalk in Santa Cruz.

Just before they passed onto the bridge, Robin scooted towards him on the front seat, then reached across him to pay the toll taker. She passed her bare arm so close he could discern the scent of her pale white skin. She stayed right beside him even as they crossed the bridge. He put his hand on her knee, and she moved closer until she was right up against him.

As they zigged through the psychotic city streets, she told him about things she'd kept secret: her waking dreams, her out of body experiences, flying over the city. When Joey unlocked the steel door at Time & Space and opened it, a heavy blast from Paula and the Pistols stopped them dead, pushing them back a step.

Robin shouted to be heard above the electric force field.

"There's something I want to show you." She took his hand. "Don't be scared."

She led him down the concrete steps into the musty basement of Time & Space. Iron-black pipes crisscrossed the ceiling. A rusting boiler dripped red-brown water. The freight elevator shaft bottomed out here, in a graveyard of broken bits of sheetrock, shattered glass, plastic jugs, empty paint cans, odd lengths of wood, and the old, broken television Sheila had tossed down the empty shaft.

"I come down here to meditate sometimes, or read," Robin said.

There was an old mattress and box spring laid out in one corner, a half-broken little table stood by it with a desk lamp on top. They sat down on the mattress, side by side. She told him more about seeing the slender, dishwater blond woman in the mirror that spanned the sinks in the industrial strength bathroom. She told him about Madge in the dreamy kitchen, and the little tow-headed boys playing with fire trucks on the floor. She kissed him.

"What about Mac?" he said.

"He never comes down here. Nobody ever does. Except us."

twenty-three

Another Friday morning. Robin was in her every-day, morning panic. When she dashed through the orange-carpeted living room, she was already smoking her fourth cigarette. She envied Zumpo as he snored away under the spotless, aluminum ping-pong table. He was like a child, or so she imagined, unconcerned with worka-day things like bosses and buses. The simple thought of those two evils made her run double-quick and fly down the concrete stairs impervious to the dangers of the plunging elevator shaft.

Outside, the Troll shouted his usual threats, but she was out of breath and had to slow down to a walk. The only thing that kept her going these days—grinding her life away in a paper mine—was the promise of a week long vacation scheduled to start on Monday. She didn't have enough money to go anywhere but, figuring in the weekends, she would not have to go back to work for nine whole days.

It was September, and the City's weather was always warm in September. She couldn't jet off to Rio, but she could get some sun on Time & Space's high, flat roof—at least enough so that people at work would stop remarking on how pale she was. Relax, kick back, get some sun. As she hustled down Natoma, she imagined herself and Joey—why not Mac?—bicycling through Golden Gate Park, the last vestige of nature in the relentless gray of the constricted City.

Just down the alley Robin saw a new arrival in wino paradise. A woman sat, hunkered down against a concrete wall. Her legs were drawn up. Her arms held the knees close. A watch cap was pulled down over her ears, and she rested her forehead against her knees. Fetal position, Robin thought. The woman raised her head, and Robin stopped dead in her tracks when she saw it. The woman could have been her twin: dishwater blond hair, thin face, high cheekbones, pale skin. She was like the reflection Robin had seen months before in the cracked mirror in the industrial strength bathroom.

"What the hell are you lookin' at?" the woman said.

Later, after work, when Robin returned to the Natoma, she looked for the woman. But the woman was gone, and Robin felt an unsettling sense of loss.

That evening she cooked meatballs and spaghetti for her housemates while the news ran on the television in the room of the orange carpet. As usual, the volume was turned up as high as it could go but, still, she could only hear pieces over the angry rock of the Roily Bitches and the feedback from their Strats and speakers: the Summer Olympics in Montreal, race riots in South Africa, a tsunami in the Philippines. Sheila had bought another day old white cake for dessert, and they ate that in the orange-carpeted living room while they watched Sanford and Son—"Well, Judge, if that's the case, forget the divorce, gimme the gas chamber!"

Mac lay stretched out on one of the two couches, his arms locked behind his head forming a pillow. When a commercial came on, he rotated his body and head so that he managed to look at Robin.

"Go get us some more wine, will you?"

The future flashed through Robin's mind at a million miles an hour: a one room apartment in the Tenderloin, cheap red wine, black and white TV, spaghetti and meatballs.

"You don't mind, do you, sweetheart?"

"It's getting dark, *sweetheart*," Robin said. "And I don't want to go down that fucking alley alone."

To no one in particular Mac said, "I think I'm in trouble." He rose to a sitting position on the couch and counted the house: Robin, Zumpo and red-haired Sheila McCarthy.

"Hey, Zump'. Be a good fellow and walk my wife down to Livpreet's, will you?"

Robin wanted to slit Mac's goddamn throat.

Zumpo crawled out from under the spotless aluminum ping-pong table.

"I got to walk off all that food," he said. "Too much luxury makes Zump' a dull half-breed." He bowed towards Robin. "It will be a pleasure to escort you, my lady."

Mac stood up, dug into the pocket of his Levi's, and pulled out some crumpled up bills. "And get some chips, too. Munchies. You know."

Down the concrete stairs again, but with Zumpo this time—past the yawning shaftway on the third floor landing, then a right turn, then past the shaftway on the second floor landing.

First floor: Roily Bitches, pierced noses, cheek rings, tongue studs. They stood silent while a joint was passed around.

Once, the one with the green mohawk had shown Robin her knife. She'd pulled it from a sheath clipped to the inside of her boot. "It's a real Luftwaffe dagger," she'd said. "I got it in Amsterdam, cost a fucking fortune."

Robin didn't care about the dagger; it was the Amsterdam part that bothered her. She'd never been outside of California except for Reno and Tijuana, and this twenty-year-old mohawk-haired freak was a fucking world traveler.

Outside, the late summer sun had left the sky. Only a dying glow remained. Robin locked the steel door with a quick twist of her key. When the lock clicked, Roily Bitches started up again—"You slit your wrists you stupid bitch …"—and a plague of blue-bodied flies flew out of a dumpster that sat on the sidewalk by the steel door.

As they walked towards Livpreet's store, Robin asked Zumpo about the woman she'd seen.

"A woman wino?" he said. "No, no woman around here that I ever seen."

The red-nose wino sat perched on the Goodwill loading dock: wine bottle in a paper bag, legs dangling over the edge, dirty and drunk. Zumpo asked him if he'd seen a woman along the Natoma.

"I saw one once. Totally, fucking crazy." He tipped his baseball cap to Robin, made a broken-toothed smile and apologized for the obscenity. "Sorry, lady."

As they walked Zumpo asked Robin why she wanted to find the woman.

"I don't know, maybe buy her some food," she said.

Zumpo, being a man, asked her if the woman was pretty.

"Hardly," Robin said.

At the corner store, Zumpo chatted with Livpreet while Robin squeezed loaf after loaf of sourdough bread until she found two that were soft and fresh. She grabbed a box of Triscuits and some cheese and a big package of olive loaf. She didn't have enough hands to carry so many groceries, and she ended up pressing them against her chest, until she got to Livpreet's counter.

As she dropped the box of Triscuits there, as she laid the olive loaf and cheese down, Robin realized that what she wanted to find out was how the woman had come to be along the Natoma. Had she been married? Had she had a husband who beat her? Had she lost her job and been unable to pay the rent? Had she been an alcoholic who had become homeless, or a homeless person who'd become an alcoholic?

By that time, Zumpo was, once again, telling Livpreet how he'd once coached offensive line, back at his old school, Gardnerville High. "But they found out I never graduated, because I got expelled for throwing a book at a teacher. They told me to go back to the reservation." He shook his head. "White people."

"They don't like Sikhs much either," Livpreet said.

"They even made Cleopatra white," Zumpo said.

"Elizabeth Taylor."

Outside, in the little park across Sixth Street, a dozen sad faced men leaned against the pastel colored conduits, listening to a preacher who was out to collect lost souls. Thinking the woman might be among them, Robin and Zumpo crossed Sixth after they left Livpreet's instead of going back down Natoma. Robin had the Triscuits, the cheese and the olive loaf in a big paper bag. Zumpo carried the sourdough bread in a bag in his right hand and the heavy jug of wine in his left, using only a single finger passed through the round glass, finger handle.

The preacher, young and black, stood on a bench so that his head was a foot or two above all the other heads. He was clean and good-looking and wore a green, army fatigue jacket. He had one glass eye and one real eye, and when the real one moved, the glass one didn't, and Robin wasn't sure if he was looking straight at her or straight through her. Sometimes, Robin feared that Christianity was a lie. Sometimes, she feared it wasn't.

The preacher was wild and angry now. He held a black Bible in his right hand, and raised it up high.

"Jesus said, 'Cleave the wood and I am there; lift up the stone, you will find me.'"

One of the sad men, wearing two layers of black overcoats, started shouting. "Bullshit. Shit and bullshit. No Jesus I ever seen. Shit and bullshit. Not down here. No Jesus around here."

The other men laughed and sipped the Night Train they'd bought at Livpreet's. The preacher kept trying. "His Kingdom is all around you. His Kingdom is you. There is nothing that is not God."

"Shit and bullshit." The over-coated man, in a boxer's stance now, threw punches at the air, at the waking street lamps, the dying sun. He danced down the walkways throwing phantom punches. It frightened Robin. There was no place for a woman here.

"We'd better go back," she told Zumpo.

The lost souls parted as the over-coated man came towards them. Silently, they began to walk away looking back over inward-turning shoulders. Robin and Zumpo started across Sixth Street, back towards home.

"No!" the preacher called. "Don't run away. We have food down at the Mission. We have clothes. Come down to the Mission. We have food for the belly and food for the soul."

As they walked, Zumpo saw the woman, pushing an empty shopping cart up the sidewalk, towards Mission Street.

"Hey!" Zumpo said. "She looks just like you."

Robin turned towards the plodding woman. "No not much. I don't think so. Superficially, maybe."

But it *wasn't* superficial. Robin *knew*. The woman looked exactly like her, and more important the woman *was* her. Or what she would become, if she didn't make changes.

The Tenderloin, black and white TV, and spaghetti seemed preferable in comparison.

twenty-four

It was four a.m. in the City, and everything was shut down tight. The bars had closed long before. The theaters and restaurants had all locked their doors. Two Doggie Diners, one on Sloat and another on Van Ness, stayed open for business all night. In front of them, their trademark seven foot tall, Dachshund heads rotated on tall white poles.

Market Street, wide and cavernous, was dead empty. Its old office buildings had become haunts for musty things. Beneath them a single, brightly illuminated trolley bus rolled down the street. The bus was empty, but as it came to Sixth Street, the driver, a bored black man with a graying goatee, saw two white men. They emerged from the cold shadow of the sidewalk's nooks and crannies. The dark one wore a heavy navy blue pea jacket so dark it blended into the night. The other one, the blond-haired one, wore a lighter quilted jacket but struggled along limping.

The driver moved his right foot off the accelerator and braked with such practiced skill the bus drifted to a stop right in front of the two men. As they stepped aboard, the driver laid his hand on top of the farebox.

"This one's on me gentlemen," he said. The men, surprised, thanked him and moved towards the interior of the empty bus. The driver, looking for some entertainment, floored the accelerator and, a moment later, hit the brake, throwing both men off balance.

Mac Jenks raised his right arm, grabbed at the handrail above and, still off balance, swung on it like a trapeze artist. Joey Wooten, who was on another binge, reacted too slowly and could only manage to fall into one of the vacant plastic seats. The wound on the left side of his face had not healed properly. Instead of flattening and blending into his cheek, it had grown big, fat and ugly. Mac, the ex-Vietnam hospital orderly, had told him to get injections of cortisone in the scar to make it blend better with the rest of his cheek.

Mac brought it up again as they rode the bus.

"I don't like shots," Joey said.

"You're acting like a child. If you get rid of the scar, you'll look a lot prettier. Robin will like it."

"What the fuck does that mean?" Joey said.

"Nothing," Mac said. "Just that Robin will like it." He shrugged his heavy shoulders. "Sheila too, I suppose. That's all I'm saying."

Mac had his little Colt .22LR stuck in his belt, behind his back, under his navy blue pea jacket. It was loaded but the safety was on, with an empty chamber in line with the barrel. Mac had lured Joey along on this little jaunt down Market by filling him full of tequila and convincing him there was a certain curiosity here he ought to see.

A few blocks later, they were walking the sidewalk in front of the Palace Hotel. The windows on its Market Street side displayed the goods of the high priced shops that leased space in its interior: expensive chocolates, Spanish leathers, alpaca clothing, ballet slippers and red shoes.

"Vulgar," Mac said. Joey asked him where they were going. "Just a little farther," Mac told him.

At the end of the block, they crossed New Montgomery at a blinking yellow caution signal, and a few steps later they stood in front of the Army Recruiting Office.

"That?" Joey said. "You wanted me to see that?"

"No, this," Mac said.

He pulled the Colt out from under his heavy coat. He cocked it and fired a shot through the front window of the Army Recruiting Office. He cocked and fired four more times. It was crazy, he thought, certifiable. Like being afraid to shave with a blade.

twenty-five

More and more Robin stayed away from Mac and the rest of them by hiding in the musty basement with its black iron pipes, its rusted, water dripping boiler. She hated it all now—Mac the lazy bastard she'd supported for so long, Sheila who was fucking him, Joey who had been making excuses—the proverbial headache, she supposed.

She was sick of the alley, sick of the Troll, sick of the hook-handed pervert who liked to wave his dick at her. She was sick of Time & Space and roaring bands, sick of making dinner and playing ping-pong. All she wanted was to get some money together and get her own little place, a quiet place somewhere. Maybe on a corner above a little grocery store like Livpreet's.

She still liked Zumpo, free and easy. He'd helped her drag an old recliner down the concrete stairs into the basement for meditation. The recliner was broken, like everything else along the Natoma, and couldn't be raised from the reclined position.

"Aren't you supposed sit on the floor," Zumpo asked, "like some Yogi Buddha lotus blossom? Legs crossed? Back straight?"

"Madeline says a comfortable chair is best."

"That's what I thought," Zumpo said.

Now, almost daily, Robin sprawled in the broken recliner drinking wine and doing psychic meditations with her crystals. She kept earplugs in her ears to keep the roaring bands from penetrating her clear calm. Once she held a tray on her lap and tried to bend spoons like she'd seen Uri Geller do on TV. Once she crumpled up pieces of paper and tried to move those. Sometimes, between meditations, she would study one of Madeline Dove's books, or one of the Maharishi's to learn about release.

Now, Robin and Madeline sat together in a small, upstairs room at the Berkeley Institute for Paranormal Research. It was Madeline's private study. Big, green palms reached out and touched each other from two of the corners. Robin loved those, but the rest of the room was garish—all red and gold and copper colors. Candles and incense burned everywhere. The incense made Robin sneeze and her eyes water. She had to ask her to put the incense out.

The two of them sat at opposite ends of a yellow couch with teak legs. Madeline had one of her legs tucked up under herself for support because the couch was so wide, and she was so short.

"If you're sincere in this," Madeline said, "it will come to you all at once. But you have to get your life right first."

"I'm quitting drinking," Robin said. She really meant it this time. No tippling. Not even Colt 45.

"Don't say quitting drinking," Madeline said.

Robin corrected herself. "I've quit drinking, and I'm quitting smoking, too."

"Maybe do just one at a time, one then the other. And you and Mac?"

"Things are about the same."

"I have a group class that can help you. Psychic Meditation. Wednesday evenings, 7 to 9, for eight weeks."

"Anything on weekends?" Robin said.

"I'm sorry. I understand how busy you are. But it's better to take as much as you can all at once. Immersion, you know?"

"The classes are so expensive."

"Yes, but you don't have to pay all at once. You could pay in installments."

Now, Robin sat in the old recliner in the musty basement of the rusting boiler, the black, overhead pipes, and the empty elevator shaft. She had a can of Coca-Cola on the concrete floor beside her, and Sheila's old, cat-clawed heating pad wedged between her aching back and the recliner. She had felt poorly the last few days, alternately sweating and shivering. Headachy. She'd gotten lost in the Consolidated Bank building on Friday, but she supposed lots of people had. It was a maze after all, thirty-six floors of local elevators and express elevators, narrow halls and unlabeled doors.

Her eyes were closed. She was grounded all the way down to the center of the earth. She concentrated on her breathing, but just as she was drifting, drifting, drifting, a sudden jolt at the bottom of her spine woke her. At first she thought the heating pad had given her a shock. She heard a voice behind her, loud and crisp, crackling like cellophane—"Fetch."

"What?" Robin said. Her heart raced. She summoned up all the pluck she could muster and looked back over her shoulder. She saw herself standing there: dishwater blond hair, high cheekbones, but worn out and pale as a ghost.

Her twin said, "I'm your fetch."

Robin didn't understand. "Fetch?"

"Apparition. Doppelganger. Fetch."

The congested, round orifice in the middle of Robin's forehead opened, and comprehension surged into her frontal lobe so fast she couldn't separate one secret, sacred truth from the next: up was down, two and two made five, all time existed at the same time, the future created the past. She became confused and frightened. She turned in the recliner and faced forward again thinking she would run, but the apparition, the doppelganger, the fetch, materialized in front of her and blocked her escape.

"Why are you doing this to me?" Robin said.

The fetch shrugged its shoulders. "Why not?"

It began to move away from her, but it didn't walk. It floated away, drifting towards the empty elevator shaft. When it turned its back to Robin, she saw that a thick black fracture ran all the way from its neck to its lower back.

"What-d'-ya-think of that?" her fetch said. It hung suspended in the empty shaft for a moment. Then, like water, it lost whatever substantiality it had and trickled, oozed, streamed down the shaftway into the pit of the broken sheetrock, the odd pieces of wood, the shattered TV.

Robin pushed herself out of the recliner and stumbled towards the concrete steps that led up and out of the dead, dusty basement. When she reached the first floor she had to stop and catch her breath. Four band guys in black leather jackets stood on the low stage. The leader, a bleached blond girl singer, stood at a keyboard. The blonde pulled the black shawl she wore tighter around her bare shoulders.

"It's always so cold in here," the blonde said.

"Yes, always," Robin told her. She started up the gray concrete stairs towards the second floor, leaning heavily against the gray concrete railing because her back was beginning to hurt.

The blonde gave the band a downbeat. "One, two. One, two, three, four ..." The band kicked in, and she began to sing. "We're so vacant but oh so pretty ..."

Mac stood on the second floor landing, watching Robin struggle upwards. She stopped three or four steps below him, breathless again. "Are you alright?" he said.

"I'm fine," she told him. She could have told him about the fetch, but he wouldn't have believed her. No such things, he would have said. It was just a dream, he would have said, a hallucination brought on by drinking too much cheap wine.

"So where the fuck is Sheila?" she said.

twenty-six

It was nine p.m., and the party at Polluted Press was starting to howl—Bobby Sun and Blues Dragon. Usually reserved, Bobby let his hair down, literally, for gigs. No horsetail tonight. His hair, no longer confined, flowed down over his shoulders, between his shoulder blades and down his spine.

"If you seen my little red rooster ..."

He shook. He riffed. He knelt and bent his head down so far that his waterfall of black hair rolled back over his head and covered his face. Bobby's wild-eyed Vietnamese drummer: shaved head, gold tooth, nose pierced with studs like stars. One foot thumped the bass drum. The drumsticks in his hands rattled the snare. He swallowed the microphone on the stand by his face and sang harmony.

"I'm that little red rooster too lazy to crow for day." Everyone knew what "little red rooster" meant.

The bass player, a kinky-haired white man, bounced bass lines off the balls of his feet. In high school he was tall enough to play power forward. Now, his platform shoes made him two inches taller.

"If you see my little red rooster please drive him home ..."

The concrete floor had been cleared for dancing—everything in this neck of the woods was concrete—but it was early yet, and a single, lone, undulating woman had dared venture onto the dance floor. She stretched her bare arms high above her head and swayed back and forth in time with some silent, distant music.

Robin Jenks, lean and pale, stood away from the empty dance floor and the crowd that milled around it, posturing on its edges. Robin had a paper cup half full of beer in one hand and a smoldering cigarette in the other. Her back was pressed against a wall display of the graphic novels and the underground comics Polluted Press published: sex, drugs, violence, horror. The cartoonist who drew "Road Kill," Teo Rodriguez, faced her now. He kept one hand up against the display rack, cutting off her retreat. He shouted in her ear but, even so, she could barely hear him over Bobby Sun's roaring rock.

"You're from across the street, right?" Teo said. "I see you going to work sometimes. Coming back. Whatever."

He was good looking, tall and fit, with long hair that was well kept and clean. His shirt was half open exposing some of his chest and abdomen. It was rather lewd, Robin thought, but captivating, too, and she couldn't stop her eyes from snatching glimpses. He had a nice tan for a cartoonist, at least, but that, she supposed, was just a sunlamp illusion.

He bent slightly at the waist and turned his head so Robin could shout directly in his ear. Their heads bobbed up and down, a human mating dance, like long-necked birds she'd seen on some TV show. The intimate, heart to heart talks, she desired weren't possible when amplifiers were turned up all the way and ears were stuffed with jangle and ringing.

"We've said hello a couple of times in Livpreet's store," Robin told him. "And at the last party."

All he wanted to do was fuck her, of course. But she had worn her tightest blue jeans to show off her long legs—the only form of communication possible at a thundering party at Polluted Press.

"Yeah. Yeah." Teo jokingly banged the palm of his hand on his forehead. "Of course. It's Robin, right? Real laid back all the time."

"Laid back?"

"Yeah, you know. Relaxed like nothing ever bothers you."

"Not exactly," she said. She thought she was wound up tight, if anything.

"You're married to the guy who wants to be a comedian? Right?"

"*Wants to be,*" Robin said, letting contempt roll off her tongue.

Teo asked her how she liked living on Skid Row. "It must be especially hard, for a woman I mean."

"It's not so bad. I have a place to live, at least. It would be awful if I had to sleep in the alley and push a shopping cart and beg for money. I mean, how can anyone, especially a woman who might get raped or murdered, stand that? I'm afraid I won't be able to if the time comes for me. And I know it will come if I don't get out of here. I've had a sort of premonition, you see ..." She realized she was starting to sound crazy and stopped herself short.

"I'm sorry," she said.

"Hey look." Teo had a fake schoolboy smile on his face. "I'm out of beer. Can I get you some more?"

"Oh, I can get it myself," she told him.

"Nice talking with you," he said. "Maybe we can have a dance later?"

"That would be nice," she said, but he was already walking away.

There was a big, silver beer keg in back where the printing presses were. A few moments later, Robin went to refill her cup and maybe catch up with Teo, but he wasn't there.

Sheila was in the crowd that huddled around the keg. "I see you've got your hooks into Teo Rodriguez," she said. "A real looker and he's got money too."

"Him?" Robin said. "We were just talking."

"It would do you some good, don't you think. I mean nobody is monogamous anymore. Right?"

By now a few people had become drunk enough to start dancing. Sheila took an exaggerated deep breath, exhaled hard and took the plunge.

"See you later," she said.

Sheila slithered up to the best looking guy in the vicinity, but Robin stayed by the keg, drinking beer and smoking. When nobody asked her to dance, she felt like she was in high school again and decided to move on. She climbed a concrete stairway not much different from the one at Time & Space. On the roof she found herself in a little clutch of pot smokers. Mac wasn't there, but Joey and another guy were firing bottle rockets at the winos in the alley. Every time one whooshed and popped, a wino jumped, and the spectators on the roof laughed and cheered.

A woman with orange hair passed her a joint, and Robin took a long toke and passed it along. When Joey saw her, he left his bottle rockets behind. He came up to her, threw an arm around her waist and pulled her towards himself.

"No," she said.

He kissed her on the lips anyway.

"Nobody will see," he said, pulling back. "Mac's playing ping-pong."

They kissed again and this time, she let his tongue come inside her mouth. She felt the kiss all the way down to her privates, and she tightened her arms around him, drawing him even closer.

They clung to each other for a moment, until Joey said, "Later," and went back to his bottle rockets. She sucked down more pot when a black man wearing a Giants cap passed her a silver pipe. The pot took her hard, now, and she felt like she was going out of body. Only empty, night sky was above, and the thought of the void scared her.

She began to walk back down from the roof on the wide, concrete stairs. Zumpo, cleaned up, smooth shaven, and wearing "new" clothes from Goodwill stood on a crowded landing holding forth for a blond-haired California girl.

"Our hunting grounds were stolen from us," he told the girl. "Our pine groves were cut down to shore up the white man's silver mines and stoke the fires in his stamping mills ..."

Robin gave him a sly thumbs up, and Zumpo winked back. She found the room where the Polluted Press ping-pong table stood. Spectators leaned against the walls drinking beer and smoking, cigarettes and pot both. She hid among them, lit up a cigarette herself, and watched as Mac dispatched some déclassé hippie who still wore love beads.

"Next victim!" Mac said.

Everyone laughed when Mac missed a ball on purpose and did one of his Chaplinesque pratfalls.

"So go fuck Sheila," Robin thought, leaving.

She flattened herself against the stairway wall to make room for a bearded cartoonist whose name she couldn't remember and his pudgy little girlfriend. Not an appealing couple, but even though the two weren't married they'd been together almost forever. Robin smiled and said hello as they passed, holding her beer high so it wouldn't get knocked out of her hand.

"Anybody at the ping-pong table?" the cartoonist asked, and she remembered that his pen name was Peter Rabbit and that he drew bondage comics.

"I'm jonesing for some ping-pong," Peter Rabbit said.

"Mac's been holding the table," Robin told him.

"Not for long!" Peter Rabbit said, and they all laughed.

Now, Robin stood in a long line along one edge of the print shop, waiting for her turn at the one and only bathroom. The woman in front of her passed her a joint and told her the line was so long because people were really using the bathroom to snort coke.

She said her name was Sweet Jane. "You know, from the song. 'Livin' on reds, vitamin C, and cocaine.'" Robin took her for a dingbat.

"You can go in with me, if you want," Sweet Jane said.

"But I've got to pee for real," Robin said.

Sweet Jane told her she could do that too. She smiled and laughed. "Did anyone ever tell you that you looked like Viva?"

"Lots of times," Robin said.

"You live in the building across the street? Right? The one that's haunted?"

"Haunted? Why do you say haunted?"

"Joey told me."

Adrenalin shot through Robin's beating heart. Her spine prickled. "Joey? What did he say?"

"Oh, that the place is riddled with spirits. Demons in mirrors. Ghosts in the kitchen."

The little back-stabbing bastard.

"He's cute, too," Sweet Jane said. "And that blond hair. He must use conditioner, don't you think?

"I'm sure I wouldn't know," Robin said. "And I don't believe in ghosts."

"Oh, I do. Believe me, I do," Sweet Jane said. "They're all over around here. Just go out in the alley."

"The winos, you mean?"

"Some of them are possessed," Sweet Jane said. "And I mean that literally."

Later, flying high on Sweet Jane's cocaine, Robin danced with Teo Rodriguez in the dead center of the concrete dance floor. There must be a rush to betrayal, she thought, a rush as thrilling and powerful as the rush of love.

When Teo took her upstairs to show her his studio, she knew what that meant. He chopped up four lines of coke. After they'd snorted them, Robin felt like she was flying for real. She swooped around the room, left and right, arms stretched straight out like a kid playing at being an airplane. Finally falling, half on purpose, she landed in Teo's arms.

She had a particularly vivid dream that night in Teo's bed, a drunk, high, confused dream. It was not her flying dream, not a dream of an infrared gull swooping through the city. Instead she dreamed she was fucking a ghost. His arms were warm and soft around her. His ectoplasmic tongue slid down her throat into the pit of her being.

In the morning Robin dressed quickly and left Teo's room while he was still asleep. In the alley the Filipino wino who had hooks for hands somehow got his dick out of his pants and waved it at her. She turned her head away and just kept going. An older woman pushing an empty shopping cart came towards her. She looked like Madge: fat, pale, coughing. Her hair was tangled. Her left eye was swollen as if someone had punched her.

"Spare change?" she said.

"I don't have any," Robin told her.

"Got a cigarette?"

"I'm all out."

"Your name is Robin, isn't it?" the woman said.

Robin freaked. "No," she said. "Get the fuck away from me!"

Robin stumbled, nearly falling, but she made it to the steel door that kept the demons out. She unlocked it and slipped inside. The first floor was empty and for once, silent.

No bands yet, thank God. As she climbed the concrete stairs, she started thinking up excuses to tell Mac. She hoped he'd be sleeping off a drunk himself so she could quietly slip into bed without him even knowing. As she climbed the last concrete step and crossed the orange carpet she decided—fuck it, maybe I'll just tell him the goddamn truth.

But when she opened the bedroom door all the lies she'd made up flew right out of her head. Mac was sitting up in bed with a bottle of cheap red wine laid on her pillow beside him.

"You're fuckin' Teo now? I knew you were fuckin' Joey. But I didn't know you were peddling it all over town."

"I never fucked Joey, you know I never fucked Joey."

"You fucking whore. At least make 'em pay. Get out of my sight you slut. Go fuck Teo. Go fuck Joey."

He leaned over the side of the bed, picked up a tennis shoe and threw it at her. It hit her hard and knocked her shoulder back.

"No, you get out," she said. "I hear you when you're fucking Sheila, you goddamn pervert. Hypocrite. Vietnam, big fucking deal. Grow the fuck up. Learn how to shave."

twenty-seven

George Zumpo figured he was on the road to redemption, a possibility that frightened and confused him. The white man's mores had entered his life so completely that he had begun to drink socially acceptable wines. But one day, when summer was ending and the autumnal equinox neared, he grew sentimental about the good old days and so became, for a short time at least, a lapsed model citizen.

Zumpo went outdoors and visited his old haunts. He crawled under the Goodwill loading dock and had a long conversation with the Troll regarding the merits of various budget-priced wines and liquors. There was nothing like Cisco Red they agreed, and after they shared a couple bottles of the stuff, the Troll got to work. He set himself up mid-alley in a boxer's stance—much improved since Zumpo had taught him the basics—and issued his usual challenges to some hallucination or other.

"What-d'-ya think? What-d'-ya-think of that?"

Zumpo, short on funds, was Cisco-ed up enough to consider robbing Livpreet's store but instead settled for panhandling. After a hard day's work—"Spare change? ... I need twenty-five cents carfare so I can visit my poor, little, leukemia-lized son in Oakland ... I haven't eaten in three days ... Baby needs a new pair of shoes ..." Zumpo was able to collect enough lucre to buy two more bottles of Cisco Red.

Later, he lay stretched out on one of the tattered couches in the orange-carpet room watching the Johnny Carson Show. He was wrapped in a purple comforter that leaked white cotton batting. He had slept earlier but in a Cisco Red punctuated sleep, turning over and over again, sometimes half off the couch, sometimes half on.

When Johnny signed off with his patented club-less golf swing, "Goodnight everybody," Zumpo realized he had to pee. A black and white American flag came onto the screen and Kate Smith sang the Star Spangled Banner. Zumpo sat up and pondered his options. In an earlier time, he simply would have peed on one leg or other of the spotless, aluminum ping-pong table, but he was no longer a barbarian.

He seized the remains of the Cisco Red, and Zumpo, the great walker, stumbled towards the industrial strength bathroom. When he found it, he switched on the lights and unzipped his Goodwill-new blue jeans. He filled one of the urinals with foaming gallons of yellow pee, while emitting groans of pleasure. When he was done, he let his dick hang out of his jeans to cool it down and went to one of the three sinks to wash his hands. He looked into of the big cracked mirror and took a glug from his bottle of Cisco Red.

"Mirror, mirror on the fucking wall ..." he said, just like Robin, but no apparitions appeared. He only saw himself, a once free man who was now, essentially, a Rez Indian. He considered heaving the bottle of Cisco at the mirror but then thought better of it. He could just as well heave the bottle at the mirror after the rest of the wine was gone.

"Waste not, want not." It was a thing Rez Indians said.

He started back for his couch in the orange-carpeted living room but became disoriented and when he reached the doorway, he turned left instead of right. Steering an erratic course down the narrow, sheet-rocked hall he came to a dead end in the cockroach-infested kitchen. He couldn't find the light switch. He sat down on one of the chrome and vinyl kitchen chairs that surrounded the tin-topped table and tried to figure out why he was there. He began to hear opera, *Turandot*, floating through the dark kitchen air and drunkenly assumed some fly-by-night opera company was rehearsing on the first floor. Now, when he took a swig of the Cisco Red, it tasted more like Vino da Tavola. Then he smelled his Sicilian grandmother's meat sauce—beef, veal, bacon, onions, carrots, celery, tomato purée, red wine.

Zumpo's brain rotated 360 degrees inside his skull, and Mama Giulietta herself appeared. Ancient and stoop shouldered, dressed all in black, she stirred a huge cauldron of meat sauce that bubbled on the stove. She turned and looked at him.

"Why you been tellin' lies about me, Georgie boy? Pahrump, for Chrissakes. A '59 Imperial? And how come you didn't have the decency to come to my wake?"

Zumpo mumbled, "I think I was in jail."

"That's what you always say Georgie boy, and it's crap. You didn't come to my wake because you were too chicken to look at a dead woman ..."

"I tried, *Nonna*."

"The devil take you, and stick your pee-pee back in your pants. What the hell you got your pee-pee hangin' out for?"

The kitchen began spinning, and Zumpo's head began spinning in the opposite direction. He breathed once and tried to speak but passed out instead.

twenty-eight

It was a warming Saturday and Indian summer ruled the City. Robin stood on the wide roof of Time & Space with one foot on the low, concrete curb that guarded the precarious edge. Exhaust fumes poisoned the air. The city snarl rumbled like the sound of creation. Looking over the edge, down into the alley of speeding Chronicle trucks, winos and detritus, she imagined swimming down through the snarl of fumes until she went splat on the asphalt.

She moved back towards the center of the roof and sat down on the edge of a beaten up, outdoor chaise. She wore a navy blue, two piece swimsuit that made her look even skinnier than she was and did nothing to disguise her pale white skin. She squeezed Sea & Ski suntan lotion into one hand and spread it over her shoulders and ashen legs. She lay down on the chaise, but raised her thighs and bent her knees so that they formed an inverted V—tidy and safe.

There was an uncanny silence directly below her, inside the cold concrete of Time & Space—no bands today. The water heater had died completely, and today was the day Mac and the rest planned to raise the new one up through the elevator shaftway all the way to the third floor.

Robin opened her copy of *The Teachings of Don Juan.* She wasn't quite sure she believed it all. She actually felt better since she started drinking again. She had a can of Colt 45 set down on the roof in easy reach. It was idiotic, she'd realized, for Madeline Dove to have told her to stop drinking and smoking. In Castaneda's *Teachings*, they'd eaten peyote buttons and smoked jimson weed, so why not Colt 45 and tobacco?

A crash, like stars colliding, came up from the great below. She heard shouts—"Holy shit!" that was Zumpo.

"Is everybody okay?" that was Mac.

It was predictable, of course: Mac, Joey Wooten, Zumpo and Bobby Sun, ropes, pulleys, block and tackle, a water heater that weighed a ton. What else could one expect?

She grabbed her terrycloth bathrobe, slipped on her sandals, and went down the fire escape to the third floor fire exit at the back of the cockroach-infested kitchen. Once inside, she found Bobby Sun, smelling like marijuana, standing on the third floor landing, looking down the empty shaftway.

Before she even had a chance to ask, he said, "Damn! I never saw anything like it. Whoosh, right on down! Damn, that thing was heavy!"

Robin grinned. "Pretty cool, eh Bobby?"

"Yeah! Wow! Whoosh!"

Robin moved to the dizzying edge of the shaft, steadied herself against the concrete wall and looked straight down. Mac had strung work lamps all the way down the shaftway. The back of Zumpo's head stuck out over the opening on the second floor landing. Joey's blond head stuck out on the first. Mac was down in the very bottom of the pit inspecting the damage.

He called out, "The thermostat got sheared off, and it's got a couple of pretty big dents." He looked up at Robin. "Sorry kiddo, still no hot water."

The condescending bastard.

That night, Robin and the rest watched television, drank wine and smoked weed. She wanted to get away from them and get into the basement and meditate, but Mac and the others had been teasing her about her "hallucinations" ever since Joey, the little bastard, had betrayed her trust at the Polluted Press party.

Mac said that she had so much caffeine in her that she didn't walk in her sleep anymore, she ran. When he cracked a water heater joke, "I'll try to fix it, but it's a *tankless* job," it seemed so silly that all of Robin's tension flowed right out of her. She began laughing and couldn't stop.

"I didn't think it was that funny," Mac said. That only set her off again and, pretty soon, everyone was laughing at Robin laughing.

It was a good party that night, the wine glasses were always full and there were chips, dip and chocolates. They played ping-pong and smoked more weed and watched television—Bob Newhart—while Roily Bitches roared in the rehearsal space below.

"You goddamned punk you stole my junk ..."

They called out for an extra-large pizza, and when it came they had a little feast in the room of the orange carpet and watched The *Mary Tyler Moore Show* on TV. Robin sat on one of the saggy couches with her back supported against the arm rest and her legs and feet up on the cushions so she faced the television. During a commercial for Kentucky Fried Chicken—"Gee Mom, it sure is neat to have you at the table instead of at the stove"—Mac stood up and pulled some crumpled up dollars out of the front pocket of his Levi's. But he gave them to Zumpo, instead of Robin, and told him to go down to Livpreet's and buy some more wine.

Sheila said, "And some chips and chocolate chip cookies, maybe."

Zumpo asked Robin if she wanted to go with him. She just said, "Thanks, but no," and shook her head. *The Bob Newhart Show*, about the funny psychiatrist, was just about to start.

Bobby Sun said he'd go too. "You know, man, to help you carry."

They finished the old jug by the time Zumpo and Bobby Sun came back with two big jugs of wine and all the chips and dip they could ever eat. Sweet Jane—from the Polluted Press party—came flying in on Zumpo's arm.

"Look what we run across in the alley," Zumpo said. "You guys all know Jane, right?"

All of them said hello at once. "Hey Sweet."

"How you doin', Janey."

"What's happening, Jane," Robin said. Sweet Jane had shared her cocaine with her at the party, and Robin thought she liked her. But later, Teo Rodriguez told her that Jane tried to communicate with the dead.

"On a Ouija board," he'd said.

"Does it work?"

Teo had just shrugged his shoulders. "*Quién sabe.*"

Now, the wine flowed. They finished the chips and dip and the last slices of pizza. They played ping-pong, smoked weed, watched television and ate white cake with plastic forks off paper plates.

Sweet Jane said that she could feel vibrations everywhere.

Mac wisecracked again, "It's the Roily Bitches playing *molto fortissimo* is all.*"

"No, no. This place is overrun with psychic energy. I can feel the vibrations."

Jane stood in the middle of the room moving her hands in flat circles in front of her, as if she were trying to feel the texture of an invisible wall. She walked down the narrow sheet-rocked hall running her hands along the thin, vulnerable walls.

Robin's neck and shoulders tensed. The muscles pulled up tight, and she couldn't get the taste of plastic forks out of her mouth. She drank more wine and shrugged her shoulders trying to ease the cramping. She moved her head in circles around her neck and wondered if anyone heard her vertebrae crack. Sweet Jane was a dingbat, she told herself, and Madeline Dove was just after money like Mac said—buy another book, take another class, have a private consultation.

Newhart was almost over by the time Jane came back—*All in the Family* was next. Robin tried to concentrate, but there was too much noise—Roily Bitches, ping-pong, Sweet Jane's endless chatter. She turned on the couch and resumed her earlier position—feet up, back braced against the armrest, facing the television. All she'd ever wanted was a family.

"Paranormal phenomenon everywhere," Sweet Jane said. "Transcendent phenomenon."

Mac, who was playing ping-pong with Joey, stopped without warning, and the ball bounced past him.

"What the fuck does 'transcendent phenomenon' mean?"

"Something spiritual is all," Jane said. "Something outside the physical universe. Zumpo saw a ghost in that very kitchen. A *real live*, well dead, ghost."

"I see pink elephants sometimes," Zumpo said. "Like when I overdose bad wine. But I see shit when I quit too, like the DTs."

Mac started cracking ghost jokes. "Why do ghosts make bad liars? Because you can *see right through them.* Ghosts always appear *right before someone screams.*"

"Nobody ever died here," Joey said. "At least I don't think so. It used to be a print shop ... But before that ..."

"It doesn't matter," Sweet Jane said. "Ghosts can haunt people, not just places, and sometimes, what people call ghosts aren't ghosts at all, but emanations from another time or dimension."

"We could hold a séance!" red-haired Sheila McCarthy said. "I've got a Ouija board!"

Sweet Jane drew in a lung full of air. "We shouldn't. Because it isn't a game, you know. We might encounter an unclean spirit, a demon or maybe even the devil."

"If we do," Sheila said. "We'll just tell it to relax and have a drink."

"A succubus would be okay," Mac cracked.

Robin grabbed her wine and cigarettes, stood up and walked to the door of her bedroom.

Sheila said, "Don't you want to play?"

Play, Robin thought. Drunken children playing house. That was all they were ... all she was. She began to feel sick from the white cake and the wine and the chips and dip.

"No. It's okay," she said. "I've got a little headache is all. I think I'll just go to bed."

She stepped into the tiny bedroom—a king-sized bed that was way too big, a wardrobe that was way too small, an old wooden rocker, a lamp, bedside table and her clock radio. The Bitches' music still rumbled up from below. The thick walls of concrete only served to channel the piercing music up the concrete stairs. The ping-pong games, the television, the chatter from the orange-carpet room went through the thin sheetrock as if it was not even there.

If she ever needed some help to get to sleep, it was now. She lifted up a corner of the king-sized mattress where she had hidden her bottle of little red pills and took two. She got under the bed covers, waiting for that wonderful moment the pills gave her—like falling into something, flying up to something.

How stupid she'd been. She'd wanted to believe so badly that there was something beyond City snarl and drudgery, something better than a loveless marriage. But it had all been dreaming, sleepwalking, alcohol, cocaine, the DTs. There was no astral plane, no pie in the sky, just a fucking bunch of winos in a fucking concrete alley.

The pills took her, and a pair of warm, loving hands embraced her. It wasn't Mac. Mac wasn't warm and loving. It wasn't blond-haired Joey Wooten. Joey Wooten was rushed and greedy. The hands rolled her onto her back. They massaged the inside of her thighs.

"Who?" Robin said.

"Your fetch," came the answer.

twenty-nine

Mac dreamed of sunshine filtering through his bedroom window. Warm on his face, warm on Robin's, but it was a dream of richer times. When he woke, he dragged his left hand across his face to smooth away his swollen sleep. The warm sun wasn't there anymore. Robin wasn't there, either.

He lay on his side, on a couch, in the orange room. Zumpo snored his life away on the other. The television had been left on all night. Mac, rose to a sitting position and realized his temples ached, and a pulse beat in his eyeballs. Standing made it worse. He bent his head forward and took three experimental steps towards his bedroom. When he reached it at last and opened the door, Robin wasn't there. The bed had been slept in. He assumed that she was up and about, probably in the industrial strength bathroom shivering in a cold-water shower or in the kitchen boiling water for coffee. He quickly slipped into the much too effeminate, chinoiserie robe Robin had given him one previous Christmas.

He didn't find her in the bathroom shivering in the cold-water shower. A stray thought tickled his brain—he should hang doors on the partitions that divided off the toilet stalls. Nothing fancy, just some plywood, some light hinges, some little barrel bolts to ensure privacy.

Now, he imagined Robin standing in front of the old moaning refrigerator, sleep-eating Sheila's day old white cake. He stumbled down the sheet-rocked hall to the kitchen, but she wasn't there either—not at the fridge, not sitting at the tin-topped table. He felt miserable, dehydrated from all the alcohol he'd drunk the night before. Finding a glass that was almost clean, he rinsed it out and filled it with cold water.

Then the obvious occurred to him. He stepped back down the hall. Adrenalin shot through his body. His face and brain filled with hot blood. He threw open Joey's door and flipped on the overhead light.

"Where the fuck is she?"

"What?" said Joey, woken from his own hungover sleep.

"My wife, you goddamned coward. Where's my wife?'

Joey shielded his eyes from the light and braced himself on one elbow. "Why would she be here?"

"Why the fuck do you think?"

Back in his own room, Mac slipped into his Levi's and an old bulky sweater he especially liked. He raced down the concrete stairs, past the empty shaftway, into the thick-walled second floor—darkroom, gun range, black metal desk. He opened the center drawer of the desk and took out the little Colt .22LR. He flipped open the loading gate and stuffed six copper plated bullets into the cylinder. He put it on half cock and stuck it in his waistband under the bulky, gray sweater.

Down the stairs. Out the front door. Same old alley. Same old winos, crouched against walls, huddled in doorways, lying flat on the sidewalk, smelling of urine.

Mac, in his rage, had forgotten to put on shoes and, as he crossed Natoma, the raw asphalt cut his feet. He tried to open the door at Polluted Press, but it was locked. He rang the bell but nobody answered. He pounded on the door and leaned on the bell, until finally, Peter Rabbit—the one who drew the sex comics—unlocked it and opened up.

"Hey Mac," the Rabbit said. "What's up? Kind of early for you, isn't it?"

Mac didn't like Rabbit, and he realized, now, that he didn't like any of them.

"I'm doing great, Rabbit. How are your fuck books selling?"

"They're erotica, not fuck books."

"Sorry, Rabbit. Erotica." Mac pushed past him into the open space that fronted the print shop. "Is Teo upstairs?"

Mac didn't wait for Rabbit's answer. He dashed up the concrete stairway and opened the first door he came to. Some burned out hippie whose name he didn't remember—Ziggy maybe—was in his underwear, getting dressed.

"Sorry," Mac said. "I thought this was Teo's room."

"Next one over," Ziggy told him.

Mac went to Teo Rodriguez' door. He tried it, but it was locked—or latched probably, with some cheap little flip-lock. He broke right through it, hard and fast, and the cheesy little lock snapped. Teo was naked on his bed enjoying his morning jerk.

"Mac?" Teo let go of his dick. Mac pulled the Colt, and the dick instantly shrank to nothing.

"Where the fuck is she?" Mac demanded

Teo sat up in bed and gathered the dirty, stained blankets to hide his privates. Mac stepped towards him and stuck the gun right up against his dick.

"Where the hell is my wife. You were fucking her weren't you?"

"Christ no. I don't know where the fuck she is."

"Stay away from her," Mac shouted, "or I'll blow your goddamn balls off."

Mac crossed back over Natoma. His bare feet were bleeding now. He passed through the wino gauntlet—Swollen-Nose, the Troll, the hook-handed Filipino. Down the alley, he saw Bobby Sun walking towards him carrying two guitar cases—his Strat and his old Epiphone. Mac shoved the Colt back in his belt.

"Hey Mac, you don't got any shoes on."

"Robin disappeared, and I can't find her," Mac said.

"Disappeared? Like UFOs or some shit?"

Mac unlocked the steel door, and the two went inside. Mac told Bobby Sun that he'd looked everywhere for her. "I don't know. She's fucking everybody, I think." Hot blood blew through the top of his head again. "You haven't been fucking her, have you?"

"Hey man. Take it easy. Maybe she went to Livpreet's for some female shit or something."

"Yeah, Livpreet's," Mac said. He turned away from Bobby, and noticed the stairs to the basement. Of course. It was Sunday, and Robin was down there, hiding from this old, wrong-turned world. She was probably lying in that damn recliner, earplugs in her ears, half drunk on morning wine.

Mac went down the short flight of stairs calling her name. "Robin! Goddamn it, answer me!"

But when he had barely entered that hellish quarter of rusty boilers and black piped ceilings, he saw that the recliner was empty. Unable to stop his churning brain he had an awful vision of Robin sleepwalking the concrete stair, across the smooth concrete landings where the scant barriers of one by fours no longer stood. Two endless seconds later he found her.

She lay stretched out on her back at an angle across the broken water heater. Below her was all the garbage they'd thrown down the shaftway when Time &

Space was new and fresh: the odd pieces of sheet rock, the old shattered TV set, the paint cans, the plastic buckets, the detritus of life.

He stepped down in the pit and went to her. Her arms, stiff and frozen, were stretched upward as if she were trying to latch hold of something high above. She had no pulse. Her skin was cold and rubbery. Her eyes were dilated.

He had barely known her, a pretty bank teller cashing his check, a lover, a wife. He kept his composure. He went back upstairs used the phone then returned to her and cried.

When the emergency medics finally came, one of them slid into the pit and looked into Robin's wide-open, blue eyes. The other medic, a chubby little man with a fifties style, ducktail haircut, asked Mac if he wanted them to work her up.

"I don't know what that means," Mac said.

"Try to resuscitate her," the ducktail said.

Mac said, "It's way too late."

"Just checking."

Ducktail told him that he probably didn't want to watch what they were going to do next. Mac nodded his head, for he knew they were right, and climbed out of the pit.

thirty

After the medics took Robin's body away, and the cops left, Zumpo followed Mac, Sheila and Joey Wooten up the concrete stairs to the orange-carpeted living room. They sank down into the deep, musty couches.

"Life goes on," Mac said, so they drank cheap red wine.

They turned on the television because the rehearsal studio was vacant, and they missed the noise. When the television didn't distract them enough, Sheila suggested they play Hearts because it would give them something to do with their hands, so they played Hearts.

In the early evening, Sheila ordered food from their favorite Chinese restaurant, but the restaurant refused to deliver.

"You've delivered here before," Sheila said.

A Chinese sounding voice said, "The boss' son was shot over there. You want food, you come get."

Nobody, and especially not Mac, wanted to drive Robin's car, but Zumpo, the great walker, volunteered to go.

Joey Wooten objected, "It'll be cold by the time you get back."

Zumpo was offended. "Don't worry. I walk fast."

"We can heat it back up," Sheila told Joey.

"That'll ruin it."

"Shut up, Joey," Mac said, and Joey shut up.

Zumpo put on his Salvation Army greatcoat and his black Stetson with the eagle feather in the headband. It was an easy walk up Mission Street to the restaurant, and he did his best to avoid thinking about Robin. Instead, he thought of pot stickers, Mongolian beef, house chow mein, garlic stir fried broccoli, and steamed rice.

Just inside the restaurant, there was a glass counter with souvenirs for sale. Behind that was the kitchen—ovens, stoves, steaming pots, flying grease, cooks, noise and confusion. A fat Chinese waiter wearing a dirty white apron over a belly so big it made him look nine months pregnant, walked out of the kitchen and greeted Zumpo at the cash register.

"What you want?"

"I come to pick up our order."

"Not ready yet."

Zumpo said, "We called it in an hour ago," which was an exaggeration, but he was turning into a white man, and white men lied all the time. So did Chinese men and even women, he supposed.

"You sit down, hold onto your potato."

"Potato?" Zumpo said.

Without answering the waiter turned away and walked back into the steaming kitchen, loaded five or six dishes of food into a dumb waiter, then said something in Chinese to the cooks. The cooks laughed. Life goes on: Mongolian beef, house chow mein, garlic stir fried broccoli and steamed rice.

A couple of aging, artsy hippies, a man and woman, walked down the creaking stairway that led to the second and third floors where the dining rooms were. The waiter re-emerged from the kitchen steam and took their money with hungry grins and patronizing "thank-you's."

As the two left, Zumpo called to the waiter. "It's under the name Sheila McCarthy."

"Don't let go your potato," the waiter said.

Life goes on.

At last, and after negotiating the purchase of a big paper bag to hold all the little paper cartons of food, Zumpo began to hot foot it for home. He kept the paper bag right up against his chest so his body would help keep the heat in. He walked so fast he didn't have time to peruse any of the fascinating sights along the way: the Fifth Street Parking Garage, the Hotel Zenda, the State Employment Office.

As he climbed the concrete stairs he heard the jolly whacks of ping and pong—life goes on. But as he entered the orange-carpet room Mac slammed his paddle down, hard, on the aluminum ping-pong table.

Mac: "What the fuck, Joey? Play right."

Joey: "I am playing right. And it wasn't my fault, it was yours!"

Mac served the ball so hard it barely caught the back edge of the table. Joey got to it, turned his paddle as he captured the ball, and fired it back as hard as he could. Topspin.

From one of the old, sagging couches Sheila called out, "Come on, guys. It wasn't anyone's fault. It was an accident."

Sheila had set plates, knives and forks, and paper towels for napkins on the same coffee table where Mac usually ground down cocaine.

"It's still hot," Zumpo said. He cast a hopeful smile in the direction of the aluminum ping-pong table, but it didn't slow them down one bit.

"And how the fuck could it be my fault?" Joey said. "You were her fucking husband. You ignored her cries for help."

"Cries for help, my ass. Some goddamn fake psychic? Is that a cry for help? You're the fucking adulterer."

"So what have you and Sheila been up to?" Joey said.

Mac threw his ping-pong paddle at Joey so hard that even Zumpo ducked, then Mac stomped towards the door and the concrete stairs.

Joey shouted after him, "She didn't fall. She jumped!"

Zumpo got the Chinese to Sheila, who shoveled a couple pot stickers onto a plate and scooped some dipping sauce on top.

"Come on Joey," she said, holding out the plate like a lure. "Come on. Calm down and eat. You'll feel better."

Joey hobbled towards the two of them shaking his head. "He's fucking crazy." He dropped onto the couch like the fall of a heavy blade and took the plate from Sheila.

"Goddamn him." Joey pulled on the back of his neck like it was stiff with pain. "Do you know what he did to me up on Market Street? Did he tell you about shooting out the window?"

"Look out!" Zumpo said, for at that moment, Mac came through the doorway, that little Colt in his big right hand.

Sheila got to her feet. "What the hell? Mac?"

The Colt cracked loud for so little a gun, and Zumpo heard a little bee sizzle passed his ear. Joey was on his hands and knees, by now, between the couch and the coffee table. Mac pulled the trigger again and paced slowly, deliberately towards Joey.

"You fucking coward," Mac said. Zumpo got over the initial shock of the whole insane scene and tried to grab hold of Mac's right arm. When he failed, Mac pointed the gun towards the ceiling and pulled the trigger, but the gun clicked empty.

"She didn't jump, you motherfucker. She fell! Now get the fuck out of my house you little twerp."

"It's my house as much as yours," Joey ventured.

"I'll fucking kill you if you don't get the fuck out of here."

thirty-one

Alone at the edge of a narrow beach that was far from the City, Joey Wooten drank from a screw top bottle of cheap pear wine. There was a party going on in one of the ritzy houses just above the rental cottages that lined the beach. He could hear the sounds of drunken chatter and laughing. The air smelled of barbecue, seawater and twilight. Water snaked through the black, half broken pilings of the old, wooden pier that ran a few yards out into Monterey Bay.

This was one of his old haunts. Not as crowded as Cowell, and the surfing could be easier here for a guy with a fucked up left foot. He'd come back to it all—the ring of the pinball machines in the Skee-Ball parlors along the Esplanade, the chatter from the party, the smell of burning meat, the rock jetty where the surf broke.

He took another drink of wine. Robin always told him that he drank too much, that they all drank too much, but tonight he wanted to melt into oblivion. That was the clean way to put it.

High hopes had turned obscene: alcohol, infidelity, death. But had she jumped? Hell, he didn't know.

He started walking down the beach keeping to the edge of the foaming surf. He stopped and took another glug of wine. Summer rentals climbed the hillside at the edge of town. Just above those, richer homes watched the sea and sand.

There came a leftwards bend to the beach here, leading to the jetty of low, black rocks where the best surfing was. But tonight the seawater rippled easy in the light of an ascending moon. He trod carefully on the tops of the wet rocks but his left foot and his special shoe caused him to slip twice. He nearly fell.

A certain measurable impairment had come over him but nothing like oblivion.

Beyond the jetty were the Capitola Bluffs, like cliffs, that defined the back edge of the long, narrow beach. Sinuous red-brown kelp stalks, alien things, stretched across the sand towards the bluffs. He'd been told more than once that the smooth, slippery pods at the end of each branch contained fresh, drinkable water. But they seemed such unworldly specimens he'd never been brave enough to find out if it was true.

Instead, he crushed as many pods underfoot as he could.

He heard a voice. "They don't like that, you know."

A girl emerged from the murmuring surf. She wore a two-piece swimsuit—a kid, twelve years old maybe, thirteen at the outside, and even skinnier than Robin. Her wet feet looked silver in the light of the moon.

"They don't like being stepped on," she said again.

"I didn't think they did," Joey said. "But they're dead, so what?"

"They've just been stranded. By the last storm." She pointed at the bottle of pear wine that peeked out of his jacket pocket.

"Can I have some?" the girl asked. Joey told her she was too young. "I'm eighteen, and my parents let me drink wine."

"Yeah right, eighteen," Joey said. A wise-ass kid was the last thing he needed. Still, he gave her the bottle, and she took a tentative swallow.

"Ugh! Why do you drink crap like that? Good wine is good, but crap is crap."

"I said you wouldn't like it."

"No you didn't," she said. "You just said I was too young, which is all relative anyway." She pointed down the beach. "Did you see the porpoise?"

"The porpoise? No, I guess I didn't."

"Come on!" She began to trot down the beach. She looked back towards him once then shifted into high gear. "Come on, it's down here!" Her skinny legs flew left and right, and she kicked up sand with her silver feet. Joey wasn't sure if he was feeling paternal, pedophilic, or just plain drunk but, whatever the cause, he hobbled along after her.

She stopped, finally, where a beached porpoise lay on the thick, wet sand just beyond the reach of the lapping surf.

"Isn't it awful," she said. "Just isn't it?"

Its back was gray. Its eyes were frozen.

"Dead as a doornail," the girl said. "If it hadn't beached it would be belly up in the water, like a goldfish."

She sat down cross-legged about ten yards from the creature and patted the sand next to her. "Don't be shy," she said.

"What if it's diseased?" Joey said. "I don't think we should get that close."

"It's not diseased. It's starved. Can't you see how emaciated it is? The bay is mostly fished out, and there isn't enough for all of them."

Joey's instincts told him not to, but the girl was between him and the creature, so he sat down.

"Like this," she said. "Lotus Position." He attempted to bend his knees flat and cross his ankles just as she did, but he listed drunkenly to the right and went over onto the sand.

"You're silly," she said.

Joey got back into the Lotus Position as best he could, and they sat like that, right next to each other, quiet and bathed in the silver light of the moon. Joey drank his wine and was relieved that the girl didn't ask him for more. He asked her how she knew so much about porpoises and fisheries.

"I swim with them sometimes. There's still some in the harbor. They like me. Listen to this." She began making clicks and hums to demonstrate how she and the porpoises sang to each other. Joey thought it a pretty poor imitation and didn't believe any of it but, still, he kept his mouth shut.

"It works better underwater," the girl said.

He was slouched in the sand cross-legged, now, a poor lotus flower indeed.

"Look ..." She scrunched her skinny butt into the sand and readjusted her feet and ankles. "Try it again. You don't have to be very good at it just yet, but you just can't quit."

She leaned towards him and spoke as if she was imparting a secret. "Just don't fall over again. Got it?"

She was the most devilish little wretch he'd ever seen but, despite himself, he gave it a try.

"Lotus Position," she said again. "From India."

He couldn't get his right foot much past his ankle, so he tugged at it until his knees made a crack. He started to tilt right again but stuck out a hand for balance.

"See. You're getting better already," the girl told him.

Joey tried to assume an attitude of nonchalance and cracked the other knee. "I once knew a woman," he began again, "who went to India to look for God."

"Did she find Him?"

"No. It was too dirty for her. Flies."

"She should have swum with the fishes instead," the girl told him. "I can't dive anywhere near as deep as a porpoise, but I can hold my breath for maybe five minutes."

"Five minutes! I don't believe it."

"I've been timed," she said. "But only underwater," she added.

The girl began to tell him a rather odd story about a drunkard who was captured by pirates. The pirates ended up throwing him overboard. "But you know what? A porpoise—a dolphin, actually—let the drunk ride him, or maybe her, all the way back to shore."

"Ah, an allegory," Joey said. "And I suppose I'm the drunk?"

"If the shoe fits ..." She stopped herself. "Sorry. What happened to your foot?"

"An accident," Joey said. "Bad luck."

They talked a while longer until the silver-footed moon dropped from the sky. The seaward wind kicked up its heels and tangled the girl's hair. Joey had finished his wine, and the shy warmth of evening had passed. Venus was in the sky, and the girl pushed herself up off the sand and told Joey she ought to be getting home.

"Maybe I could give you a ride. I have a car. Where's home?"

The girl waved a hand towards the bluffs. "Oh, it's just up there." She gave him a little peck on the cheek then ran towards a flight of concrete steps that wound up the bluff side. He looked away for a moment, towards the darkening sea, and when he turned back she was a will-o'-the-wisp and already gone.

He lifted the screw top bottle to his lips and tilted it up as far as he could. There was always a drop or two left in a bottle of wine, but this time there was none. He sat for a few minutes longer, stargazing. He stood up so abruptly that the stars seemed to reel across the boundless night. He fell again into the soft, forgiving sand.

Still, he needed a drink.

thirty-two

A day or two after Robin's death, Zumpo went to Livpreet's store to tell him what had happened. He didn't suppose Mac would do it, or Sheila.

When he entered, Livpreet put his hands together and made a little bow as had become tradition. "Go 'Niners," he said.

Zumpo made a little bow in return as he always did. "Gene Washington is my savior."

He told Livpreet that Robin was dead and how she had fallen down the empty elevator shaft. Livpreet could only shake his head.

"I saw police cars," Livpreet said. "And the paramedics ... But this life isn't real, you know. It's all just a dream."

"Maybe so," Zumpo said.

He told Livpreet he was going to leave the City as soon as he tied up some loose ends. Livpreet said he wouldn't miss Zumpo one bit, and Zumpo smiled and told Livpreet he wouldn't miss him either. They shook hands and said goodbye.

Later, Zumpo stuffed all the clothes he couldn't take on a walkabout into a shiny black trash bag. He carried that to the SOMA Mission and passed the clothes out to the sad men who were already lined up there.

He told Pastor Huang of Robin's death just as he had told Livpreet. Pastor Huang said she had gone to a better place.

Zumpo said, "No, she's dead."

He aimed to walk across the Golden Gate Bridge and head north. He had not been on a long walk since coming to the City months before. He needed to get himself in better shape as he had grown fat on three meals a day and snacks. He did some panhandling on Market Street to raise funds for the expedition.

"Spare change? I need some money so I can walk to Ketchikan and visit my brothers the Tlingit."

Most of the white people and black people, the yellow and brown people he appealed to just walked past him, heads down to avoid his gaze. Many others seemed to decide he was a lunatic, and some even crossed the street to avoid him.

A French woman shook his hand. "Walk to Alaska? You're one crazy Indian."

The next day he panhandled his way out into the Mission District and out towards 22nd Street. He found himself standing at 2786 1/2 22nd Street, and pushed the doorbell. Charlie Weasel answered.

"What do you want, George?"

Zumpo was tempted. He could have wisecracked, "To show you my ass," but he kept himself respectful and genteel.

"I would like to talk with you about White Dog."

He heard Leela shout, "Tell him to go away."

"I didn't come to see her," Zumpo said. The words tangled in his mouth like snakes. "It is time we smoke the peace pipe."

"You have one handy?" Charlie Weasel said.

"Man to man," Zumpo said. "I'd like to talk to you about White Dog."

The very next morning Zumpo and White Dog began their northward trek. Mac had stayed in his bedroom since Robin's death. He'd come out to talk with Robin's family on the phone and to talk with a detective named Friday—"No relation," Friday had said. And he came out to say goodbye to Zumpo.

"If you ever come back ... well, we'll be in the book."

"Ketchikan or Bust!" Zumpo said.

The two of them shook hands. "I hope you make it," Mac said.

Zumpo and White Dog began their long walk by going along the Embarcadero just like any other pair of tourists. There were many people along this track so, although he hated to do it, Zumpo kept White Dog on a leash. He wore his Salvation Army greatcoat despite the warm October weather—"White Man's Summer." His black Stetson sat atop his old *Wa-She-Shu* head, sporting the same old, eagle feather he'd gotten at "Buy-Sell-Trade-Pawn" in Reno. But now he had fine walking boots—army surplus. Joey Wooten had gotten them for him before Joey headed south.

Zumpo and White Dog stepped along at a respectable rate of speed until they reached a place called the Marina Green. It was full of white people playing with Frisbees or playing volleyball, and many more simply lying upon bath towels trying to suntan their pasty skin. Zumpo sat down on the green grass to rest and let White Dog run. He unslung his backpack—it held six cans of Budweiser, three cans of dog food, two cans of chili, his old boots, clean underwear, a carton of Lucky Strikes, a transistor radio, and a plastic dog bowl. He took a Budweiser out, pulled the tab open, and took a drink. He watched White Dog run and chase with the other dogs, intercepting a Frisbee here, a chewed up tennis ball there.

The minions of the law would have busted Zumpo if they'd seen him with a beer can, but Zumpo had learned much in the City. Sheila had given him a Styrofoam cup holder disguised to look like a Coca-Cola can, and he slipped the beer can into that.

When White Dog came back panting hard, his tongue lolled out, Zumpo reached back into his pack, pulled the dog bowl out, filled it with water at a faucet, and let White Dog drink. While White Dog rested, Zumpo finished his beer but did not open a second can.

They set off again, with White Dog in the lead. They passed by the big pretty houses of rich white people that were all stuck together, one beside the other, just like the houses on Leela's street. But these stuck together houses faced a little harbor full of white-bodied sailboats with bright blue covers on their lowered sails. Zumpo supposed an Orkin Man would have to kill many, many bugs to buy one of those.

They walked more and came to a little park with trees and grass and a comfort station. This was welcome for otherwise Zumpo would have had to pee in the bushes and some Chinese cop would probably have busted him. Wonderfully, the comfort station did not smell of urine and overflowing toilets. Instead, the invigorating salt sea air of the Golden Gate blew in through a screen window. He filled a washbasin with water and White Dog, long and lean, put his front paws on the counter and stretched his body upwards and drank his fill.

Outside, only a mile or two away, stood the great bridge with its two tall towers of gleaming orange, just like the orange-carpet room back at Time & Space. He pointed at them with an upraised arm. "That's where we're going."

White Dog barked once, as if he understood, and they began walking again, striding wide. They passed no more rich houses or pretty boats, but instead many low, strange buildings until finally, Zumpo saw an airfield full of rich people's Piper Cubs. A chain link fence guarded it, but it was only seven feet high, and there was no barbed wire on top, either. Zumpo took his backpack off, set it down by the fence and asked White Dog to guard it. White Dog consented by lying down beside it, silently, watching like a sphinx.

Zumpo cast off his greatcoat, kept his cowboy hat on, put his hand on the top rail and pulled. He worked himself up and over, but just as he landed on the other side a yellow man in yellow coveralls spotted him.

"Hey asshole!"

It was easy to clamber back over the fence again and shout insults and challenges at the yellow man.

"Your mother sucks cocks in hell!" It was an insult he'd learned from a very excellent movie he'd seen with Robin in a crowded theater on Market Street.

After flipping off the yellow man one final time, Zumpo started walking again. Soon the two of them had gone through several parking lots, up many concrete steps along a trail that ran through a scary little tunnel that reminded Zumpo of Leela. It was but a short walk from there to the great bridge and its orange towers.

Many people walked beside them now, all dressed in thick jackets, hats, mufflers and scarves as proof against the sea breezes being sucked through the Golden Gate. Cars zoomed past onto the great bridge. The fumes from their terrible exhausts made Zumpo cough and, knowing he would be sick if he kept breathing the white man's air, he took a blue bandana out of his pack and tied it over his nose, cheeks and chin.

When Zumpo and White Dog had walked half way across, they looked out over the bridge's steel railing. The fumes and the noxious jabber of the other tourists all became meaningless. The bay and the far, opposite shore opened their wide worlds to anyone who could see. The sparkling cities curved inwards towards him. He put his hands on the rail and leaned far over. White Dog raised himself up on his haunches and put his front paws on the rail just as he had done at the basin in the comfort station. Looking down ten thousand feet into the cold, salty waters, Zumpo felt unsteady and lightheaded. Many had taken the long flight towards death from this very railing.

He thought of Robin and wondered.

thirty-three

Halloween! It's Friday and it's Halloween! The usual rounds of partying that mark the end of a dreary work-week become a pagan carnival engulfing the whole City. It's Friday; it's Halloween; it's payday! In North Beach, Coit Tower, illuminated by floodlights, stands straight up on top of Telegraph Hill. In its shadow, secretaries sip wine in the Savoy Bar, a jungle of green palms and over-stuffed chairs.

"Thank God it's Friday."

"Thank God!"

Through plate glass windows the carnival passes before them. Revelers in ostentatious costumes fill the sidewalks heading for parties, looking for parties, making their own parties on corners under street lamps.

"Look at him!" A gigantic Samoan the size of a defensive tackle parades by dressed like Henry the Eighth—purple robes, golden crown. Anne Boleyn and five more wives follow behind him.

"At least she has her head screwed on straight," one of the secretaries quips. She taps on the glass. "Susan! Where are you going?"

Anne Boleyn stops gracefully and turns towards the window with dignity befitting a queen. "Paula's Party," she says. "We're going to Paula's Party."

Paula's Party! The secretary's hazel eyes grow wide at the thought of it. "Me too," she says. "I'm going too."

Anne Boleyn curtseys awkwardly then walks off behind her king.

"I don't know," one of the secretaries says, confidentially. "Anne Boleyn? She looked kind of Jewish to me."

On Castro Street, gay rebels promenade with ladies in blond wigs, five o'clock shadows and ersatz mink stoles—the Rose Parade in drag. Tourists pack the sidewalks snapping Polaroid pictures.

There have been incidents: gay bashers throwing bottles, shouting insults, starting fights. Cops try to contain the violence with nightsticks and threats. A Chinese-American cop leans on a traffic barricade chatting with leather boys—Marlon Brandos on chrome plated Harleys. Beer bottles break in the gutter. A fight. Cops steer two handcuffed fraternity boys into the back seat of a squad car.

A leather boy passes a joint to a woman dressed as a witch—peaked hat, fake nose, low cut black dress.

"I don't trust cops." Leather Boy says, "I think there's going to be a riot."

The witch tells him she is going to go to Paula's Party. "It'll be safe there ... well, maybe."

A man in a gorilla suit overhears. "Oh my, Paula's Party, oh my." Effeminate voice for a gorilla. "Paula throws the best parties."

Leather Boy takes his turn on the joint. "Wild parties, absolutely wild."

In the Laff-a-Lux a new comedian goes onstage. He mimes tripping on the cord to the microphone. There is a titter of laughter. He stumbles again, flying forward at an angle, feet churning as if desperately trying to keep from falling. He succeeds. He hoists up his pants, straightens his loose, blue blazer then falls with a bang on the stage. There is sustained laughter.

A red-haired woman in the audience shrieks with laughter and applauds. She wears sunglasses to hide the black and yellow swelling around her left eye.

A glass of a clear liquid with ice, topped by a slice of lime, stands next to the microphone. The comedian stands up in front of the microphone, takes a drink from the glass and holds it up for all to see.

"God invented tequila so ugly guys could get laid." It's an old joke, but there is more laughter. He drinks again. The red-haired woman applauds. No Vietnam stories this time, thank God.

The Golden Gate Bridge is jammed with traffic. Car after car inches towards the City. Fords filled with pirates, Cadillacs with cowboys. An icy wind, born in the snows of Alaska, makes the toll takers shiver in their booths.

On the opposite shore, a half-breed American Indian, headed north to visit his brothers, the Tlingit, has interrupted his walkabout and camped on a promontory that overlooks the Golden Gate. He drinks cheap wine and ruminates. His white dog sometimes romps the promontory chasing sea birds, sometimes barks at the cars on the great bridge, and sometimes sits quietly beside the half-breed as they keep a vigil for the dazzling, deadly, dying City.

In an alley just south of Market, the loud music coming from an old industrial building makes a dumpster buzz like a million flies. Inside is a cavernous concrete room filled with merrymakers. The music—electric and thundering—bounces off the concrete walls and sizzles skin. From a low, wooden stage Paula and the Pistols make the music of the spheres.

"One hard climb," Paula sings, her mouth loving the microphone. "One hard climb." Her voice is rich and powerful—Bessie Smith, Janis Joplin. "One hard climb to that beautiful city."

Paula—daytime waitress, nighttime singer. Paula, beautiful Paula, thirty years old and not getting any younger. She writes her own songs but nobody listens. Costumed as a vampire hungry for a meal, her face is coated with pasty white make-up, making her nearly unrecognizable.

"It's Paula all right," Leather Boy tells Witch.

The body is all Paula, can't be missed. Full hips, slim waist, breasts bulging against her black satin dress. "Lord let me into your beautiful city," she pleads.

Paula's boyfriend, lead guitar in her band, stands on the back of the low platform that acts as a stage. He stays hidden behind tiny glasses, their tinted blue-green lenses barely larger than his eyes. When Paula sings she is lost in the emotion of the song, but her boyfriend is a mechanical man. He works at his music; his riffs are correct but stolid. He is uninspired, somber.

"No soul," Henry the Eighth tells Anne Boleyn.

"I hear he doesn't even have a job." Anne loves to gossip. "She works and he spends the money. Off with his head, that's what I say."

A white woman watches alone from a corner. She wears a full length, white, backless dress. Anne Boleyn observes that her skin is so pale it's like that of Elizabeth the First, Queen of England, famed for her beautiful skin.

"Why, Elizabeth is our daughter, isn't she?" says Henry the Eighth.

Anne Boleyn thinks for a moment. "Why yes, I believe she is. But don't worry, she hasn't even been born yet."

The party boils over and leaks upwards, onto the second floor. The gorilla from Castro Street chases Faye

Wray up the concrete stairs. Next to an empty elevator shaft Amelia Earhart and Carole Lombard discuss the pros and cons of air travel. The secretary from the Savoy is a belly dancer now, clad in a halter of gold coins and transparent pantaloons that she fears are much too revealing.

Belly Dancer sees the pale woman in the backless dress standing by Carole Lombard and is drawn to her. She staggers slightly as she climbs concrete stairs crowded with a maze of costumes—a caveman in skins, a Roman guzzling grapes, Teddy Roosevelt. She touches the pale woman lightly on the shoulder but the skin is so cold she recoils.

"What are you?" Belly Dancer asks. "Your costume, I mean. My friend said you look like Viva."

"I'm a ghost."

"You don't look like a ghost," the dancer says.

"Appearances can be deceiving." The ghost raises a cigarette to her insubstantial lips, inhales, then blows smoke into the dancer's face. Belly Dancer's soul shivers.

"You're tired," the ghost says. "Here take this." She hands the dancer a small, foil packet and when Belly Dancer peels it halfway open and peeks inside she sees a half gram, perhaps, of pure white powder.

"What is it?"

The ghost shrugs her cold, bare shoulders. "Ghost dust."

The dancer pushes the packet back at the ghost and laughs nervously. "My mommy told me never to accept gifts from strange ghosts."

"Discrimination, that's all it is. Take it," the ghost whispers.

Once she had found this haunt ugly and repellent, but the ghost loves it now—the cold concrete, the musty basement, the long cracked mirror in the bathroom, the cockroach-infested kitchen. She loved the empty elevator shaft so much that nightly, she would position herself at the shaftway's edge on the third floor. She would stretch out her wispy arms in front of her like a high diver, then plunge down into the pit at the bottom: the broken bits of sheetrock, the shattered television, the fractured water heater.

"Lord let me into your crystal city."

The toll takers from the Golden Gate arrive, their uniforms serving as costumes. Standing by the steel door they listen to an angel and an astronaut argue about the face on Mars. Napoleon enters, medals filling his chest. He and George Washington discuss the use of field artillery in breaking up large masses of infantry.

Laughter. A giant phallus shooting balls of white cotton out its head has to duck to get through the door.

"Oh my!" the gay gorilla says, glancing longingly into eye slits cut just below the glans. "My, my. Biggest one I've ever seen."

"It's only paper maché," says the giant phallus laughing. "Unfortunately."

"I been workin' so hard ..." Bass player and lead guitar sing harmony. "Can't get into the rich folks yard."

The ghost appears like a wisp of marsh gas behind the band. When they stop between songs, she slips foil packets into their hands.

"Cool," Paula's boyfriend tells her.

Paula notices a long dark shadow on the ghost's white back.

"What's that?" Paula asks.

"My backbone," the ghost says. Paula laughs.

As she snorts the ghost dust, Paula notices three drag queen hula dancers grouped together, hanging back against one of the concrete walls. Sensing the possibilities, she picks up her guitar and leads the band into something strange, Polynesian and exotic. Something seductive to the western ear. The hula dancers begin dancing. Hips swaying, hands rolling like the sea, but it only takes a moment to forget those lovely hula hands. Swaying hips turn to thrusting hips, hips out, belly back, in and out. As they dance they forget everything—the boss who overloads them with work, the ex-boyfriends who threaten them over the phone, the dead feeling they have on Mondays.

Now, the belly dancer joins them. Hips and belly in and out, pressing against something that is not there. Hips and bare belly. She has never done anything like this before, never danced like this before, never made love in a dance before. The sight of her hypnotizes a high school science teacher dressed as Cleopatra, Queen of the Nile. She catches a glimpse of one of the Belly Dancer's nipples between the golden chains of her halter. It looks brown and wet like fertile earth.

"You like her?" The ghost appears beside Cleopatra and startles her.

"Yes. I like her."

"She's so beautiful," the ghost says, slipping a foil packet in Cleo's hand. "Haven't seen a body like that in centuries."

"Beautiful, yes," Cleopatra says. When the light is behind Belly Dancer, Cleo can see through her pantaloons as if she had on nothing at all. The legs are thin, so very white and somehow sad.

"Would you like to have her?" the ghost says. For a moment, the Cleo does not understand her meaning.

"Have her all night long. Five times, six times, all night long?" She hands Cleo a packet of ghost dust.

Cleo undoes the foil, looks at the powder, touches her index finger to it and tastes it. "Coke?" she asks. The ghost shakes her head. Cleopatra, the science teacher, peers at the powder and sees nothing special about it. But if she had her microscope, if she could look at it just once through those wonderful lenses her students detest, she would see that each grain is perfect. Like a snow-flake, each is unique, a wonder of the universe.

"Try it," the ghost says, "it's magic."

"Been workin' so hard." Paula keeps the band tight and fast.

"I don't think ..." Cleo begins to refuse, but the ghost's eyes drink her in. Whirlpool eyes, blue, quick-sand eyes. Ghost Dust tastes like milk and honey.

Paula tosses down a glass of hot wine while her boyfriend takes a solo. She holds her throat open so the wine runs into her like water down a pipe. Her boyfriend plays all the notes, every single one of them, but his music is still lifeless. He plays as if his fingers were wood. Paula faces him and plays along with him, trying to inspire him, but the music does not rise. It does not reach the heights that lift the soul out of the body and let it float free.

Spooks and goblins whirl on the dance floor; the music is good enough for them. Pumpkin men with green, leafy bodies and pumpkin heads join hands with cow-boys and kings all of them spinning together. Jesus of Nazareth in polyester robes jitterbugs with Mary Magdalene. A ballerina twirls on pink toe shoes. The toll takers watch, their faces still frozen by the icy wind.

"This will warm you," the ghost says, handing a packet of powder to each.

"Looks like bicarb to me," one says.

The other is knowing. "Heroin."

In the industrial strength bathroom, behind a closed shower curtain, Napoleon stands, his fly unzipped, cock covered with ghost dust. On her knees a woman dressed as a whore—red short-shorts, mesh stockings, black spike heels—lifts the cock to her painted mouth. French pastry drenched in sugar.

Another band arrives. Black men dressed in com-bat fatigues, a camouflaged Reggae band. Roadies, or perhaps only young men costumed as roadies, walk in behind the Reggae band. They carry congas, flutes and keyboard through the door. Excitement, applause.

"The Heaters," Leather Boy says. "Saw them in Jamaica. Oh what a time that was. We found this nude beach ..." Leather Boy reconsiders. "Jamaica? Maybe it was Hawaii."

Heaters' keyboard player chews an unlit cigar and puts his arm around Paula's shoulders. He speaks with a phony Jamaican accent.

"Would you like to jam with us some pretty lady?"

Keyboard Man is really from Oakland. Conga Player pulls the cigar from Keyboard's mouth and chews it himself.

"That one there," he says, pointing the cigar at the pale white ghost. "That one there, she invited us."

"I don't think I know her," Paula says.

"Nor I, pretty lady. Does it matter?"

"No." Paula smiles and laughs, "Nothing matters." It's an open party, a free party. It's Halloween and Friday and payday. Everything is open and free!

"She gave us these." Keyboard Man pulls packets of ghost dust from the pocket of his fatigue jacket. "She said it was magic. Me, I think it looks not exactly white, mescaline maybe?"

In the shower stall in industrial strength big bathroom the woman dressed as a whore swallows Napoleon's cock. "Oh God, God, oh my God." White-hot sperm spurts—bang, bang, bang—into her mouth, down her throat. She tries to swallow the cock even deeper.

Reggae beat. Paula on keyboard. The huge dance floor is so crowded people are barely able to move. Everyone dances to Heaters' Reggae—Belly Dancer and Cleopatra, Gorilla and Leather Boy, Ballerina and Toll Taker.

"You got to, got to, keep on tryin'."

Now, Paula's boyfriend plays with his soul not his fingers. His music floats free like white powdery clouds above the city. Paula closes her eyes and screams into the microphone; the dancers stop and listen. Paula throws out an old Bob Dylan song—"If you're not busy bein' born you're busy dyin'."

Belly Dancer and Cleopatra, their eyes do not meet but the warm breath from their lungs touches and draws them closer. The belly dancer takes hold of Cleo's shoulders and pulls Cleo towards her. Mouths find mouths. Tongues find tongues.

Music pumping loud. Heater's Reggae! Paula and her boyfriend play together, soaring like powdery birds. Bodies touch bodies. George Washington and Anne Boleyn unite. Toll Taker and Carole Lombard. Belly Dancer sees herself lying on her back in a field of daisies covered in ghost dust. Hips and belly in and out.

"If you're not busy bein' born you're busy dyin'." Paula and Jack sing together, throbbing metal Reggae. Electricity, megawatts of power, shoots upward like a sky-rocket and bursts into stars—brilliant white explosions illuminate the City. It's Friday! It's Halloween! It's payday!

Acknowledgments

Several individuals were very helpful to me in the writing of this novel. Thanks to Joe Towers for allowing me to use the name "Time & Space," which he created. Thanks also to fantasy writer Peter S. Beagle for his encouragement and strength, to Al Garrotto, writer and critical reader, Elana O'Loskey, newspaper journalist and editor, and James Hanna, writer of thought provoking fiction. After reading the first edition, my dear friend Eve Ness volunteered her services to correct the numerous mistakes I had made. Thank you, Eve. Finally, a huge thank you to Bryan Costales, writer, publisher, and friend without whose ideas and encouragement I never would have written this novel.